HER VAMPIRE LORD

DARK VINTAGE
BOOK 2

INES JOHNSON

Published in the United States of America

Second Edition: June 2024

1

G*aius*

"MASTER GAIUS, please may I suck your cock?"

My cock twitches in my pants, as though it will answer the woman's desperate plea. I'm only semi aroused. Most of my blood is still in my brain because my mind is elsewhere. That is why I came here in the first place; I need more blood in my system.

"I've been such a good girl, Master Gaius," says a different feminine voice from the first. "Please? Just the tip? I'll suck it so good, I promise."

I open my eyes and take a minute to focus. It's dark in the private room. I don't need much light to see. My superior sight means I need only a pinprick for me to track my prey.

They are right where I left them, inside this locked room with leather padding for walls, chains dangling from the ceiling, and sex toys littering the floor. Both women are on the floor. Knees spread. Hands on thighs, bound together with fur-lined cuffs. Nipples tight, begging for attention. The dark buds remind me of the berries that should be growing in my vineyard and my mind wanders again.

For centuries, I have been able to grow grapes in any soil I dig my fingers into, be it the briny regions of France or the saline coasts of Spain. But here, in the dry desert of southwest America, my vines are refusing to yield.

"Please, Master Gaius, may I come?"

Once more, my attention is called back to the present. I focus fully on the two women on the floor. Their bodies are trembling, like an earthquake is waking beneath them, ready to break them apart. The earthquake is a pair of Sybian sex machines.

The two women sit astride the Sybians' saddles. Nestled between their thighs is a dildo with a ribbed base that vibrates against their clit at the front and their anus at the back. The controller is set to a low hum, just enough to tease but not send anyone into orgasmic spasms. Unless the rider has been astride for a long time.

Glancing at my watch, I realize I've been here for at least a half an hour, riding these women. The scent of their sex fills the room. The air is humid with their moist juices and sweat. Their areolas are bubblegum pink and Hershey brown from the pleasure. Their labia are more red than pink from the delectable abuse of the machine.

On their asses are dark marks from the flogger I used on them. The device sits at my feet now. Hershey Brown's gaze is fastened on the device as she pants her desire for more. Bubblegum Pink's eyes are closed, her head lolling back. On her neck are two twin pricks that have puckered another shade of pink; a tiny trail of red blood meanders down her long throat.

She tasted like a stick of gum after the flogging. Sweet at the first bite, but the flavor only lasted a few moments. I liked my food saccharine. Hence, the Sybians.

The girls should now be ripe for the taking. The endorphins should have flooded their blood by now, making for a satisfying two-course dinner. But I am an admitted food snob. I like my meals cooked perfectly.

I turn the dial from low to medium. The two women mewl. They're both on the cusp of coming. Hershey Brown's eyes flash golden, her inner animal eager to come out to play.

"I'll let the last one who comes suck my cock," I say.

Their purrs are guttural. I can see their pussies shiver at the thought, then shiver in earnest as I turn the dial up to high. Their mewls sound closer to the growls of wolves. I watch impassively, my fangs twitching more than my dick. I want them in my mouth, their endorphin-rich, sweet blood. Having me in their mouths?

I give an internal shrug.

Sex has always been a game for me. One that I could never afford to lose. If I didn't bring forth the pleasure for *her*, then there would only be pain for me.

The buzzing of the sex machines pulls me back to the matter at hand. The two pussy cats are shivering, and the dial has one more setting. Asshole that I am, I switch the dial past high and wait for them to erupt.

Their mewling fills my ears. The scent of their juices fills my nostrils. The iron from their blood touches my tongue. But they hold out. I'm not sure if it's the competition between them or if they just really want to suck my cock. I don't really care so long as their hands stay bound. To have either of their claws on my flesh would bring back memories I have locked down tight.

I rise, waiting for the inevitable eruption. I think Bubblegum Pink will be the first to crash into orgasm. I loosen my belt buckle and take a step towards Hershey Brown.

A buzzing in my pants stops me. I look down at my phone. When I see the name on the caller ID, I immediately hit *talk*.

"Is she there?"

The caller doesn't even bother with hello. She has manners, I've seen them first hand. But she is a single-minded woman.

"No, Marechal," I say. "Your sister isn't here."

My brother Hadrian would never allow Carignan, his new eternal bride, to be unclothed before another. He has her locked inside his own private dungeon at our estates tonight, sating her more base needs in the privacy of our home.

"When do you expect her back?" asks Marechal.

This is the problem with turning new vampires. Humans are so connected in this new world. People text, snap, chat, and DM constantly, not allowing anyone the ability to disappear. It would all be so simple if Marechal was made to simply forget about her sister. But Cari wouldn't hear of it.

Truth be told, I don't want to hear of it either. If Marechal were mind-wiped and made to forget her sister, she would have to forget me too. Though we've only had two encounters in person, I would sorely miss the disdain and dismissal in her gaze when she looks at me.

"I need to talk to her," says Marechal in her clipped, business voice. The woman is a logical, practical, methodical scientist through and through.

I haven't seen her make a single emotional move since I met her. She never has a hair out of place, not even when her sister went missing and her brother was in an accident. Marechal had taken a deep breath, begun a checklist of what to do, and assigned each of my brothers a task. I had wanted to snatch the pad and pen out of her hand, tug at the strands of her perfectly coiffed hair, and break the buttons of her starched shirt.

But I don't play with humans any longer. They're too fragile for my particular tastes. Plus, I never enjoyed wiping their minds when things got a little rough, which they always did with me.

"They'll be back from their honeymoon soon," I soothe, lying easily.

Hadrian likely has his bride bound to a Saint Andrew's Cross and is fucking the living daylights out of her. I can't very well tell her older sister that hunch. Nor can I invite her over to see that her sister is perfectly fine, because she isn't. Not yet.

Newly turned vampires are hungry beasts. It takes a while for them to gain control over their animal instincts. If Marechal happened upon Carignan during this adolescent stage of her new life, where she is completely uninhibited, indulgent, and self-centered, it would turn out bloody.

"Where are you?" Marechal asks. "It sounds like you're at an animal shelter filled with cats."

I turn back to the scene in one of Club Toxic's private sex dungeons. I'd nearly forgotten about the two pussies on the fucking machines. They are sweating profusely as they try not to come.

"I am," I say. "I'm at a benefit for wayward animals."

"You? I didn't take you for a philanthropist."

I'm not. "I give back." I don't.

I care only about my pleasure and the wellbeing

of my family. Carignan is now part of my family. She is my sister, and I will protect her as I do my brothers.

Hmm? Does that make Marechal my sister as well?

I don't like that thought. I'm more interested in what Marechal would look like if she were on one of the machines. Riding it without a stitch of fabric on her body. Her hair down and free. Her head thrown back as I slap her nipples until they are tight peaks.

"I'm going to get off now," Marechal says, and I nearly choke. "You'll call me the moment they walk in the door?"

Oh, she is still talking about her sister and Hadrian. "I give you my word."

"I'm still not entirely convinced this isn't a kidnapping, you know."

That is another thought I like: grabbing Marechal and absconding with her against her will. Modern women say they don't like that, but the billion-dollar romance novel industry begs to differ. Women like to be told what to do. I like to be the one telling them.

"You never told me when you wanted me to come over," she says.

"Come over?"

"To look at your vine."

I've had two dripping, mewling pussies at my feet all night. But at Marechal's words, my dick goes instantly hard.

"You said it's going through a rough patch?"

"There's nothing wrong with my vine."

"You said it had rot; you showed me, remember?"

Right. She's talking about the vineyard. My pristine grapes are having trouble in the acrid, dry Tucson soil.

"The Palmezzos had trouble with that soil too," Marechal goes on. "When I was a kid, the migrants who worked the land said that it was cursed."

I am a centuries-old vampire. I have seen more than my fair share of the unexplained, and lived long enough to learn the explanation. There is magic in the world, but there is no such thing as a—

"But you and I know there is no such thing as a curse," Marechal says. "I'm sure there's an explanation. I'll be over tomorrow."

"I'll come to you," I say.

"It would be much easier if I studied the vine in its native soil."

"Too dangerous. I mean, I wouldn't want to take you away from your business."

"I do have a busy day tomorrow."

"I'll come over at sundown."

"Fine," she says. "Just let me know when you hear from my sister. And do something about those cats."

And with that, she clicks off.

I turn my attention back to the dripping pussies. Hershey Brown's eyes are rolling back in her head. With a loud thud, she falls over. Bubblegum Pink grins in triumph. I guess I'll be fucking her mouth for the rest of the evening, though my dick has softened now that Marechal is no longer in my ear.

I reach for my belt again, but a second thud fills my ears. Bubblegum Pink has collapsed on the floor, her body shuddering from a toe-curling orgasm. When the tremors stop, both women lie in comatose heaps on the ground.

I'm not put out. I call one of the attendants to see to their aftercare. Then I pour myself a glass of wine. The color is a brown that shifts to a shade of purple in the low light. It is the exact color of Marechal Durand's eyes.

2

———

M *arechal*

I FIND it illuminating that my best work is done in the dark. I was afraid of the dark at the start of my life. Even during the daytime, I found the absence of light when I closed my eyes terrifying. My mother told me that I'd been born with my eyes open, needing to see everything. It's one of the last things I remember her telling me.

That, and that I needed to take care of my baby sister.

Carignan was placed in my arms on a dark night.

As the moon had risen high in the sky, I watched my mother close her eyes for the last time. When she did, I did as I was told. I didn't take my eyes off my baby sister. I'd kept that promise for the last twenty years.

Then my dad died, the business began to fail, and now my cup runneth over.

I reach for my cell phone, to text my baby sister, to call her, to find out where the hell she is and what time she'll be home tonight. I already know that she won't answer. I know because I've been calling her nonstop for the past week. I raised her to be a little too like me: stubborn and willful, with a mind dead set on achieving her goal.

Through the window, I can see the day laborers making their way onto the vineyard. It's grape-picking season. Another bang up year for the Durand Vineyards. But will it be enough to save the business my father worked all his life to build?

My papa left the business in my hands to run. My *maman* left my sister in my arms to guide. In a matter of days, I might manage to lose them both.

Back in my room, I stare at my face in the mirror. The bags under my eyes weigh more than I do. They've been there since I was a teenager, taking care of an infant at night while going to school by day, and working in the vineyard's labs after school. Luckily, my skin has enough of the Mediterranean Sea in it that it's easy to conceal my workaholic tendencies. I balance the dark circles below with eyeshadow and mascara above.

With my face made up, I gather my dark hair into a tight bun. Using a few pins, I secure any wayward strands that dare defy the style. Doing up the last button in my starched, collared shirt, I run my hands over my fitted skirt and finally feel put together. No, it's not the most practical outfit to wear for someone who runs a vineyard, but most of my time is spent in the lab.

To complete the outfit, I step into a pair of vintage high heels. The shoes belonged to my mother. They add a touch of femininity to my boss bitch demeanor. And they remind me of the only maternal touch I've had in my life.

Both the sun and the moon are in the sky when I step outside. The sun is lingering on its way out. The moon is chomping at the bit to take over in the darkening sky.

The stems of my heels are thick enough that my shoes don't sink into the ground. I make my way down the straight lines of vines. The uniformity of the rows settles me. The plumpness of the berries makes me feel light. The fruit has ripened exactly on my schedule.

"Happy harvest, Ms. Durand."

Zahara's gaze isn't on me. It's on the berries that are about to fall off the vine into the basket she carries.

"I'm glad to see you again," I say.

Zahara and her family have been coming up every harvest from Mexico and parts of Central America since before I was born. Like most of the other migrant women, Zahara is dressed in a peasant wrapped skirt in the colors of the desert. Reds, oranges, browns, and greens. Her loose and colorful fashion is like night and day to my dark, constraining threads.

"I was sorry to hear about your father," she says, finally catching my eyes. "He was a good man."

"Thank you," I say, breaking the eye contact.

My family is not a subject I like to bring up in business. Besides, there is a lot of work to be done. It would be more efficient if I had the grapes mechanically picked. But there are some traditions I prefer to keep.

There are a few dozen of Zahara's people walking out into the rows of vines. More than the last harvest. For the first time, there are males.

"I see we have some new faces this year," I say.

One of the men looks over at us just then. He's too young to catch my interest—likely he's just out of his teens, like Zahara. But he is man enough to catch my gaze and hold it for a few seconds. There is no interest in his dark eyes. He looks away from me to Zahara. She glances down rather than holding his gaze as he approaches.

"Is the man of the house here yet, miss? I would like to speak with him about some matters." His voice is deeper than I expect. This young man probably had to grow up quickly, like me. Too bad he wasn't taught manners.

"I'm the man of the house. It's Ms. Durand. Or Boss, if you prefer."

The inner corners of his eyes pull, a clear sign of irritation. Without any further word, the man turns on his heel and walks back into the fields.

Well, if he doesn't like working for a woman, he can walk out the gate. Zahara is still on the ground, plucking away, a small smile playing at her lips.

"I don't think he'll be the one to buy me the World's Best Boss coffee mug this year," I say.

Zahara's smile grows wider, but she still doesn't look up at me. The movement lights up her face. If she ever wanted, she could be a model. Her looks are wasted in the vineyard.

Not that I would ever encourage a woman to make her way in the world on anything but her brain.

I know I have a pretty face. I look exactly like my mother. But I was always more interested in blending grapes than I was in kissing boys. Sipping at a boy's lips never gave me as much pleasure as the first sip of sweet red wine.

My phone buzzes in my pocket. I turn away from Zahara and answer the call immediately, not bothering to look at the caller ID.

"Cari?"

"No, it's me. Your brother."

I try to hold in my sigh. Arneis and I haven't been on the best of terms these last couple of weeks. He wants to sell the family business, while I've been busting my ass to save it.

"She still with that creep?"

"He's not a creep, Arneis. We both met him."

"You saw how he couldn't take his eyes off Cari. He acted like he owned her, like some *Fifty Shades* dominance crap."

This time, I do let out my sigh. I watched Hadrian Serrano with my sister. He looked lost for her, hopelessly in love. He and Arneis had nearly come to blows when Arneis had suggested they put Cari into an institution after her latest daredevil stunt. But when I saw Cari and Hadrian together, I knew her time skydiving was over. When she looked up at him, she'd seemed grounded, settled.

"I think he's good for her," I say. "I just wish they hadn't run away to get married."

"Well, that's not all he's run away with. I just found out the Serranos have bought our debt."

I go to take another step, but I can't move. My heel is stuck in the fertile ground of the vineyard. Instead of pulling myself out of the earth, I stumble to grasp onto my brother's words.

Unbeknownst to any of us, our father had taken out debt against the land. But he hadn't gone the traditional, legal route. He'd taken loans from some unsavory people. Arneis found out before I did, and tried to handle it on his own. But whenever a politician gets in bed with criminals, it's more often than not the lawmaker who suffers. Arneis's once-promising career in local politics is now on shaky ground.

"The Serranos bought five million shares in Durand Incorporated. They own more than fifty percent of the company."

Despite my heel coming free, I am still stuck in place. That simply is not possible. I had shut down all attempts for the bad seeds to buy the vineyard out. One of the local banks had given me weeks to come up with the money. By the end of the harvest, I would have it. But apparently, someone has already beaten me to it.

Not only has my sister's new husband taken her away from me, he's taken control of my livelihood. Little does he know, I am not the submissive sort. I never glance away from a man. Not only would I hold his gaze, but I'd also make him back down and give me back what is mine: my sister, and my business.

3
———

G*aius*

I KNOW I'm having a nightmare when my dick goes limp.

I'm normally in a perpetual state of readiness, even when I slumber. Legs spread, knees parted, dripping, quivering pussies come at me from everywhere I turn. My dreams are typically not much different than my waking hours. Both are filled with submissives eager for a taste of my cock.

My nightmares, when they come, are different.

Darkness falls as women close their legs. Their

cries of delight hush into whispers that are then choked into a gurgled murmur. All falls silent as she comes to my bed.

Her white hair is stark against the dark sky, rivaling the moonlight. Her long, porcelain limbs are fine and appear breakable. Looks can be deceiving. Her blood-red lips are coated with the gloss of her latest victim. It's the same red that coats the tips of her nails, which she reaches towards me.

I let my mouth slack in awe, though she's never turned me on—likely because she has a habit of digging her nails into my balls and telling me how much I love it. It took a few decades but eventually, my mind made way for that pain to become—well, not pleasure, but something less than pain. Though I never became the pain slut Domitia wished me to be.

I know that is why she likes to play with me. She wants to break me of my dominance. For centuries, I allowed her to amuse herself with my body. I allowed her to test my limits.

She is my sire. She gave me this new, everlasting life. But she never broke my mind.

In my nightmare, before she can pounce on me and ensnare me in the cock ring she uses to keep me in check, I reach for her. My clever fingers begin their magic trick as I shove all five of them into her. I work my fist like my life depends on it. Because it does.

I pump into her, fisting her roughly, just the way she likes it. In a matter of moments, she is quivering beneath me, liking the pain as much as the pleasure. Maybe a little more.

Her orgasm is long, deep. I do not stop working my hands, using my free hand to pinch her nipples, her clit, to intensify her trembling. She shudders, in the throes of another orgasm. Even then, I do not stop. As long as she's coming, she cannot strike. I do not stop until she is a quivering mess. All the while, my dick remains limp.

There's a part of me, the conscious me, that wants to wrap my hand around her throat and squeeze until her pretty little head pops off. Only, I know that she would like that. All I want is out of the nightmare. I want to wake up to a world where Domitia no longer exists.

Instead of thinking of murdering my dead sire, I think pink. Because I'm all for women's liberation. So, I think of all the pussies I've made quiver over the last month. Hell, all the pussies I made drip over the last few days should be enough to push thoughts of her pale, sadistic ass from my mind.

Once again in my dreams: thighs spread. Clitorises glisten. Nipples tighten. But there isn't much pink that I'm seeing.

I see dark skin, the color of a golden sémillon grape. As a pussy connoisseur, I know that not all labia are colored in the same shade. I know that, with the touches of honey in her skin, her pussy will be darker, likely a ruddy brown. They say the darker the berry, the sweeter the pussy juices. I'm certain that Marechal's pussy will be the sweetest I've tasted in a while.

I jerk in my sleep, but I don't wake. I've been wanting Marechal Durand for some time now. It's not the first time I've dreamed of her.

I take my time in peeling off that form-fitting skirt she likes to wear. I lose my patience at the buttoned-up shirt though, ripping the fabric apart to reveal nipples tipped with caramel morsels. The shoes, I leave on. She has a penchant for vintage French shoes. I know because not only am I a pussy connoisseur, I'm also a clothes whore. The shoes, she can keep. They'll look fantastic thrown over my shoulder as I lick her pussy.

Before I dip my head to Marechal's sweet cunny, I see a flash of porcelain in my peripheral vision. Her blood-red nails flying at me isn't what makes my blood curdle. It's that she goes for Marechal's throat.

I'm gasping for air as I jolt awake. One hand bats at a pillow on my bed. The other is twined in the sheet, ripping it to shreds.

I blink a few times before my room comes into focus. There is a light shining over me. I never sleep in the dark, even though my eyesight is sharper than an owl's.

I check every corner before I've convinced myself that she is not there. It's been a long time since she's invaded my nightmares. But over the last week, her presence in my life has returned. Not that she ever truly left the mind she'd tried to break for centuries. I may not have broken, but she's definitely left me twisted.

I rise and dress for the day. My closet spans half the west wing of the mansion I share with my brothers, and is filled to the brim with decades of fashion. My body hasn't changed in four hundred years. I could still wear the breeches made for me in the sixteenth century. Or the pantaloons from the seventeenth. Though I'm sure the mold of my dick and my ass would cause women on the streets to stop and stare. Instead of vintage French, I decide on tailored Italian.

It's late in the evening by the time I emerge from my closet and am ready to greet the night. On my nightstand, my phone is beeping. I look down to see Marechal Durand's number. My spirits instantly lift at the thought of seeing her tonight. Perhaps tonight will be the night I find out whether I'm right about the color of her nipples and pussy.

"Ms. Durand, I was just on my way over—"

"Cut the crap, Serrano. What the hell do you think you're doing?"

Not the greeting I expected. But it's been a while since I've had a challenge. I mentally adjust my timeline of having Marechal Durand's thighs open by a few hours later this evening.

"You've got some balls on you, mister."

She is right about that. Though I think agreeing with her will add a few hours to her thighs opening for me.

"First, you take my sister. And now my business."

"I assure you that your sister is fine. As for your business, I have no idea what you're talking about."

"I just learned you and your brothers bought my vineyard."

I curse under my breath. When I find Hadrian, who is likely out in his sex dungeon burying his face between Carignan's thighs right now, I'm going to stake him.

"Where are you?" I ask, already gathering my car keys to head to her vineyard. But first, I'll need to tear my brother away from his bride and see where his head was at with this decision. We don't have the capacity to take on another vineyard with this crop struggling as it is.

"I'm walking onto your estate right now. And I —ahhh!"

The sound of Marechal's scream is the last thing I hear on the line before it goes dead. But the sound is still loud in my ear. It's coming from outside, very near the dungeon at the side of the property. If Marechal happened across her newly turned sister, their family reunion would be deadly. I drop my phone and dash out the door.

4

———

M*arechal*

A SHARP PAIN radiates up my ankle after my ass hits the ground. I look down, more concerned that I've damaged my heel than twisted my ankle. I'm relieved to see that my shoes are still intact, though there are dirt smudges on the fabric.

I let out a long sigh. It's going to take me all night to get the specks of earth out. I'm usually not so careless as to walk into a vineyard in heels, but I'm not thinking clearly at the moment. What the hell am I doing out on this property in the night?

I've spent my life making rational decisions. I've had to. Women in this business aren't often taken seriously, not even when our names are on the checks.

Despite being born into the family business, I had to fight for every position, every promotion, every share I earned in the Durand Vineyard. It was no matter that my father praised every single one of my efforts. I knew I had to earn my way to gain the respect of others. And I had. Only to be handed the reins of a failing business.

I'd had no idea of the debt we were in while my father was alive. I'd woken each day and done the job I'd earned to the fullest of my abilities. I'd thought I was making strides, yet my efforts were barely making a dent in the debt. And now, it is all gone.

The hell with that.

I push up on my elbows and try to get my feet under me. But my foot doesn't budge. There is rope twisted around my ankle. I realize that's what my foot caught on, and the reason why I fell.

Who would leave rope out in the middle of a driveway?

One of the irresponsible Serrano brothers, that's who.

I've parked my car at the end of the drive. It was the only spot available after the line of expensive sports cars that scream that the owners have small manhoods. I would weep for my poor sister, but I know that the size of a man's instrument has nothing to do with his skill in using it.

The few times I've come in contact with a penis left me certain that I have no use for a permanent one. Not even one with a battery compartment. I'd purchased a battery-operated boyfriend after my last relationship fizzled. The vibrations of the sex toy had not aided in me getting off. I've never gotten off. I'm sure all the women I've seen in porn videos are just faking it.

There is no such thing as a female orgasm. It's just another lie made up by men to get women to drop their panties. Like tales of Santa Claus, or the Easter Bunny, or the Tooth Fairy: you have to be good, to give something up, in hopes that you will get a prize at the end. But I'd never had the patience to wait a whole year for Christmas presents. Chocolate eggs only lead to a trip to the dentist. Even as a child, I knew my baby teeth were more valuable than a couple of coins. So, I am not a believer.

But something about the rope against my foot, holding me down, sparks something in me. The knot that holds me still also eases something inside of me. For the first time in days—hell, it's the first time in years—I am made to hold still.

I lower my elbows down until my back is pressed against the cool earth. I look up at the night sky and notice the stars twinkling down at me. All is quiet. All is still. Something cool rests against my skin. I think it might be called peace.

The sound of a pebble kicking up and landing snaps me back to the present. I am bound, trapped, unable to rise, and something is coming in the darkness.

A figure looms over me. Broad shoulders that block out the moon and cast me into darkness. A narrow waist that extends into two powerful legs standing over me. The legs end in an expensive pair of Italian shoes that I take a moment to admire before glancing back up.

Gaius Serrano is looking down at me. His lips part into a sly smile.

I catch my breath. I'm a tall woman. I've stood toe to toe with Gaius before, and his height dwarfs me. But having him tower over me makes me feel... breathless.

I inhale, and smell the spicy scent of him along-side the sweetness of the vines. I gaze up his strong, powerful thighs, and my gaze catches on the bulge in his pants. He crouches down and my gaze stays on the bulge as it comes to eye level with me.

"Ms. Durand."

His voice is like Japanese plum wine. I hate the stuff because it is far too sweet, like confection candy. His words give me a sugar rush as his breath reaches my nose. He's only said my name, but it feels as though it's echoing through my mind. His candied tone slides down my throat and warms my chest.

"Are you checking out the competition?"

I blink. "Competition?" Does he really think his wine is at all comparable to Durand's? I scramble to get my legs under me so that I can be on a level with him. But I forget that I am trapped in the rope some careless person left out.

Gaius looks down and notes it. Something sparks in his eyes; something dark and possessive. Like he's seen his pet trying to make a break for it. I expect him to yank on the lead and bring me to heel. I'm breathless as I wait.

This is insane. I have never been on any man or woman's lead. I have always been the one holding the reins.

From his crouched position, Gaius's large hand

comes to my calf. I shiver from the heat of his touch. He doesn't immediately free me. He runs his thumb between the rope and my skin.

I forget to struggle as I marvel at the different textures of the twine and the pad of his thumb. Again, a sense of relief washes over me. All of the stresses of the day—gone. The pile of bills and notices on my desk—forgotten. The worry over my brother and sister—a distant memory.

I have the sense that if I simply stay in this man's grasp, all will be right with the world. It's the most ridiculous notion I've ever heard of in my life. I give a kick to remove his hand and loosen the rope. The rope loosens, but his grip tightens.

Immediately, I stop my motion and come to heel.

5

G*aius*

I LOOK DOWN at the treat that fate has delivered me. My incisors water at the sight. Marechal Durand is sprawled out on the ground. Her knees, which are usually trapped in her form-fitting skirts, are akimbo. I can't quite see up her skirt, but my imagination runs wild as my gaze travels up the curvy pathway of her hips.

Her chest heaves in her white blouse. The top button has come undone, leaving the lapels askew. Her ample breasts rest lopsided under the fabric.

They're practically begging my hands to free them of the bra and set them straight.

Her hair, which I've only ever seen in a tight and tame bun, has a few strands loose and around her heart-shaped face. The dark locks curl around the nape of her neck the way a tongue would sample the salty-sweetness of a trickle of sweat there.

None of that is what makes my dick go hard.

I slide my gaze all the way back down to whence I began until my eyes come to rest on the length of rope that has bound her right ankle. The strands twine from the stem of her vintage heel, over her ankle, and end at her calf. I couldn't have made a more artful design if I'd tied her up myself.

"Are you going to stand there and stare?" Marechal hisses. "Or are you going to help me?"

I put one knee to the ground, not giving a damn about the ruination of my expensive, tailored slacks. Even though I'm bent over, I still tower over her. She has to tilt her head back to gaze up at me. Her gaze is hooded in that way a woman has when she knows that a man has taken power over her.

I hold her gaze. The color of her eyes reminds me of Kyoho grape: a dark, black-purple fruit that appears fathomless. When you bite into the fruit, it's pure sweetness, like plum wine.

I can sense that a part of her is uncomfortable. Marechal Durand is a woman used to being in complete control of herself and everything around her. I can scent that she is aroused. With my expert hearing, I can hear the brush of her pebbled nipples against the fine starch of her blouse.

"Mr. Serrano?" Her voice is breathless in her attempt to be in command. "Are you going to be a gentleman and help me, or not?"

"I think I'll stare for another moment," I say.

Her gaze goes wide. When it does, I note that her eyes aren't as dark as I'd first thought. There are hints of gold at the edges, and a lighter shade of purple at the center. I've never seen the color before. I stare, mesmerized.

I reach for her—whether to lick the Sémillion gold of her skin or kiss the Kyoto purple in her eyes, I'm not sure. I'm not about to find out, either.

Marechal jerks back, away from my seeking fingers. But she can't get far. She is bound and at my mercy. Just the way I like my women.

I've never taken a woman against her will. That's not my style or my taste. I like to hold them still while I find every way imaginable to elicit pleasure from them. Most women struggle for one orgasm. With ease, I help them to find multiple releases until they are so sated from riding my fingers, my mouth, or my lash that they pass out. When they're out cold is when I like to take my due, feeding on their sweet blood from a vein in their thigh.

I already know that Marechal's blood will be the sweetest I've had in a long time. There's something about a human who was raised in a vineyard. Their very essence takes on the sweetness of the berries. Tack that on to the rush of breaking this strong, proud woman, and I need to shut my mouth before she sees just how much she makes my fangs ache.

"What are you doing?" she asks.

The crack in her voice gives away the desire she denies in herself. The flare of her nostrils let me know she wants it, even if the set of her jaw warns me that she will never ask. Fuck, I can't wait to make her beg for it.

I pull my hands away and hold them up so that she sees they are empty. "You asked for my help. I'm helping you."

She doesn't relax. Good. I don't want her to. I like her on edge. I like Marechal Durand uncertain and out of control.

I want to ruck up her skirts until I can see what she covers that sweet treasure with. Will her panties be cloth or lace? I want to tug even more strands of her hair free and set the locks loose about her shoulders. I want her back to arch as I make her come more times than either of us can count.

"Do you want me to free you, Ms. Durand?"

Marechal gulps and then nods.

Again, I reach for her. She holds still. She is stiff as a board when my fingers touch her.

I unwind the rope from her shoe and my breath catches. The rope has made a light red mark on her skin. Part of me is angry that the rope belonged to Hadrian. I want only my marks on her.

I take my time untangling her. The pattern is exquisite on her flesh. I would've thought that her honey-brown skin wouldn't mark so easily. Thank the Fates, I'm wrong. My thumb wipes over the indentations left on her flesh, and I have to bite my own lip.

"What are you doing?" she asks.

"I'm setting you free."

I deliberately rub the rope over her calf as I unwind the knot. Her lower lip trembles. Her eyelids flutter.

So, Ms. Marechal Durand has some kink in her tightly coiled person. It's always the quiet women. The ones who are the boss bitches. Put them in front of a truly dominant man, and they will open their pretty little mouths and spout the filthiest demands. Put a hand in their hundred dollar hairdo and tug, and they will drop to their knees in submission.

"You said you wanted me to help you. That's what I'm doing, Marechal. That's what you want."

"I..."

Her foot is free of the rope. She could pull away. If she wanted to.

Her eyes are wide as they stare at my hands. My fingers creep up her bared calf. If she asks, I'll say I'm checking for injury.

She doesn't ask.

My fingers make it past her knees, both of our gazes holding fast to their journey. The darkness up her skirt is allowing in a ray of moonlight. Soon, she will allow in my fingers. Then my tongue. Then I'll turn her over and make a beautiful pattern on her ass with my flogger.

"Mr. Serrano..."

I prefer women to call me *Sir, Master*. But the way she uses my surname makes my balls tighten. Role play usually isn't my thing, but I will happily be a naughty schoolboy to her disapproving teacher.

"Yes, Ms. Durand?"

"You can stop that now."

"Stop what? I'm freeing you from what was holding you back."

She gulps. Her throat works as one hand squeezes her calf and the other treks up her knee. The rope bruised her ankle, and there is a spot of blood there.

My mouth waters for it. I'm hundreds of years old, so I don't pounce on the wound. But, *futuo*, I want to sip it. This woman has me so randy, I'm swearing in ancient tongues.

"I..."

Before Marechal can get anything else out, a snarl sounds in the air, followed by a yelp, as though the one who tried to scream has been stifled by a hand over her mouth

"Is that Cari?" Marechal snatches her leg from my hold and is on her feet.

She'd fallen just outside the converted barn. The converted barn where Hadrian stores all of his favorite toys. The toy shed where he takes his new bride each night for some good ole fashioned, medieval sex play.

I'm guessing they're in there now, and Carignan has scented her sister's blood. I can't let the two see each other. If Marechal learned of her sister's dark fate, we'd have to wipe her mind. Mind wiping is a nasty business, and Marechal could forget she ever knew her sister at all. That wouldn't even be the worst outcome.

Carignan is a newly turned vampire, barely a week old. Newly turned vampires don't have complete control of themselves. If Cari hurt her sister, neither would live through it. Marechal would lose her life, and Cari could no longer live with herself.

6

———

M *arechal*

EVEN THOUGH GAIUS has slipped my foot and ankle free from the rope, I do not feel free. I can still feel the imprint of his warm palm as it pressed into my calf. The trail his fingers made as they crept over my kneecap still burns where he touched me.

His touch was light. But it weighed me down. I didn't feel trapped. I felt free.

All the weight that has been piled up on my shoulders from the year without my father, from the woes of worrying over my brother, from caring for my baby sister all these years—all of it rose from my person and dissipated into the night air. I had never felt so light as I had in the darkness.

I'd had the absurd notion to snuggle into Gaius's warm chest. To allow my knees to go slack and give him entrance. My entire body ached to go limp and allow him to carry me someplace, any place, where I no longer had a care in the world.

Until I heard the scream.

"Is that Cari?"

The sharp cry pulls me out of the insanity into which I was descending. Yanking my leg away from Gaius's hold, I rise on my own. I tug my skirt down until it covers my kneecaps and I straighten my spine.

It is Cari's voice. I know it for certain. I've heard her crying since the first night she was born, through her terrible toddler years, on into her rebellious teenage phase, up to the night our father died beside her in the car crash.

I know my sister's voice better than I know my own. I know her shouts of joy. I know her cries of displeasure. What I'd just heard sounded like one of her indignant demands.

As her caretaker when I was just a teen myself, I'd heard those tantrums many a time when we were in a grocery store trapped in an aisle where all of the candies were eye level with small children. She would ask for a treat. I would say no. She'd pitch a fit. Most parents would've given in. I wasn't most parents. I was her older sister and my will was stronger than hers, only barely. Nine times out of ten, we got out of the line and the candy stayed behind.

I hear that same teeth-clenching, migraine-inducing, patience-snatching sound now. It's coming from the structure beside the house. The stone cottage looks like a wine cellar.

I take a step towards the path. As I do, the weight returns to my shoulders. The worry reforms on my brow. The responsibility that has clung to me all of my life settles back into its place at the bottom of my heart.

Rolling my head and allowing the tendons in my neck to crackle and pop, I let the pressure fall back into place. Once it does, I pick up my pace. I need to get to my sister.

"Your sister isn't here." Gaius is at my ear, barely breaking a sweat as his long strides match my quick steps.

"You're lying to me. I heard her."

I'm at the entrance to the wine cellar. I tug at the

door, but it does not budge. I turn to face Gaius, giving him my sternest glare. This is the glare that had seven-year-old Cari getting out of bed for school in the morning. It is also the glare that had her climbing into bed at night after being told multiple times to go.

"Open the door," I demand.

"I'm afraid I can't do that."

"Can't or won't?"

My gaze narrows on him. My shoulders are square. My chin lifted. I'm giving him my full-on boss bitch stare down.

He doesn't blink. He holds my glare, gazing down at me with a look I've seen in many men's eyes: desire.

That's new. Most men back away with their balls tucked high in their scrotum. Gaius Serrano bites his lip as he leans against the doorframe, backing me into the cool stone.

"Won't," he finally answers.

"Because you're holding my sister against her will in there?"

"No." He leans into me, his voice lowered to a whisper. "Rest assured that neither I nor either of my brothers does anything to a woman that she doesn't beg us to do."

He bites his lip again. The lower one this time. Even in the darkness with only starlight to see, I can see the redness of his plump lip. His mouth tugs into a smirk as he gazes down at me.

The man is seriously handsome. The word *beautiful* could be used to describe him. He has the chiseled Mediterranean looks of my ancestors. The high cheekbones and rounded chin of the ancient Gauls. His eyes are the darkest brown, but there's a light that shines from within. It's almost hypnotic. Luckily for me, I've never been a woman prone to fall under any man's spell.

"I think you're lying to me," I say.

"*Non, minou.*"

"Did you just call me a kitten?"

"*Non.*" But he smiles as though I'm missing the punchline of a joke.

"Just tell me where she is?"

"I don't know where my brother and your sister are right now. But it's not in there."

"Prove it," I say. "Open the door."

"Are you sure?"

"Do it," I command.

Any other man would flinch. Gaius Serrano simply smiles wider, looking every bit the French version of the Cheshire Cat. He slips a key from his pocket and unlocks the door.

The door creaks open on uncoiled hinges. It is the soundtrack that starts every horror scene when the dingbat damsel runs for the shed instead of the running car. His dark gaze is a challenge.

I accept.

Turning on my heel, I walk into the door and stop in my tracks.

It's dark inside, with only a few lights. That small bit of illumination casts the space in a sepia hue. But it's enough light to see what goes on in here.

Barrels line the walls. The pleasant smell of cherry and vanilla oak is what reminds me to stop holding my breath and inhale deeply after I get over my shock. Though I doubt I will ever recover from what I'm seeing.

My brain struggles to comprehend what I'm seeing. So, I don't say anything immediately. I could be mistaken. If I am, and I say the wrong thing, I would be too embarrassed to ever show my face in polite society ever again.

Because maybe I am wrong about the contents of this room. I know the Serrano wine enterprise is ancient. It dates back to the 1600s. Perhaps they're still using medieval devices to make their wines?

But what use would they have for a Saint Andrew's Cross which takes center stage in the room? Or a guillotine with leather padding? And I've never seen a flogger being used to stomp or strain grapes.

No, this room is definitely what I think it is. A sex dungeon. I know because I've seen one before.

Not in real life. On the porn sites I checked out long ago. The only ones that ever seemed somewhat real to me were the ones where the submissive was tied up on apparatus like these, and a Dominant was taking her to task.

My breath catches. I press my thighs together. At my lower calves, I feel the spot where the rope has left a mark on my leg.

On the walls, I see a similar rope hanging loose. The memory of the free-floating I felt when trapped while Gaius loomed over me returns. Another glance at the placards of the cross, and I feel a tingle run up my spine. A peek at the flogger's tails, and the whisper of a burn on my ass flares and dies in the span of a second.

I feel a tendril of hair escape my bun and coil around my neck. My fingers tremble as I smooth the hair back into place. I run my hands down my skirt, straightening the already composed fabric.

I remember watching that video and my entire body heating. I'd only watched it the once and then deleted my browser history. It had made me feel so out of control, but I'd never forgotten the sight.

My feet are backpedaling. I need to get out of this room. When I back up, it's into a wall of solid, male warmth.

Gaius has me in his arms. His hands are a cuff around my forearms. His lips are at my ear. I can't help myself; I tremble in his hold.

7

G *aius*

I SMELL the arousal running off Marechal in waves. It's all I can do to only keep my hands on her, and not sink my teeth right into her neck. Unlike Cari, I'm centuries old and have perfect control over my hunger. But for the second time tonight, my fangs beg to quarrel with maturity.

Apparently, my dick wants a word too. It's rare that I get hard for a woman—a human, no less. I haven't fucked a warm cunt in years. I prefer to deepthroat a woman's mouth after I've rendered her cunt numb from the pleasure of my flogger. Or to get off between her breasts, after her eyes are rolling back in her head from the countless orgasms I've given her.

Marechal Durand is on her feet and in possession of all her faculties. And a human. Not my type at all. But ever since the day I met her and she extolled her belief that the female orgasm was a myth, I couldn't get the woman out of my mind.

Now I have her in my clutches, in a sex dungeon.

"What exactly kind of wine cellar is this?" she says.

As if she doesn't know. I didn't miss the recognition in her gaze as her eyes landed on the Saint Andrew's Cross in the center of the room. Or the shimmy of her ass when her attention turned to the flogger Hadrian left out.

Luckily, my stalling tactics worked, giving Hadrian and Carignan enough time to slip out of the dungeons using the caverns that ran beneath the structure. Those tunnels lead out to the vineyard, where they could resurface and head back to the house, or away into the night until Marechal is gone.

With my brother and my new sister-in-law out of

the picture, I could take a moment and strip the elder Durand down. Perhaps I could soften her up to the idea that her sister has taken on a new life. And while I am softening up Marechal, I could prove just how wrong she is about the female orgasm.

"It's not for wine," I say in answer to her question. "This is where my brothers and I like to extract a far more precious nectar."

Marechal turns in my arms. Her chest is heaving. Her plum grape eyes are wide. She tries to compose herself, but she has no idea that my predatory scent has already pinned her for an evening treat.

"This is a sex dungeon," she says.

"Yes," I agree, seeing no reason to deny it. I'm thrilled that she knows something about what is done here, and eager to gauge what she'll let me do to her here. "Would you like me to show you the process, Marechal?"

I lower my voice to a hypnotic tone that humans are receptive to. Marechal's nostrils flare, but she glares at me. She has a strong will, for a human. I don't want to enthrall her. I want her consciously begging me for it.

I want her to pull the pins from her perfect bun and let those thick tresses unravel. I want her to shimmy out of her confining skirt and open her legs to me. I want her to part those knees that are always pressed together when she walks, and beseech me to lick her dry.

"Have you brought home a treat, brother?"

I turn to find Virius standing in the doorway of the cellar. Tonight, he is dressed in a purple sari wrapped around his bare chest and a pair of red sweat pants with Adidas stripes running down each side. On his feet are a pair of my Italian loafers. I bite my lip instead of yelling at him to keep his hands off my stuff, because I need him to keep his fangs off our guest.

I put myself between Marechal and Viri. Virius is a picky eater. As far as I know, he hasn't drunk straight from the tap, as it were, in decades. Possibly centuries.

"She smells sweet," says Virius. His gaze flashes in the dim lighting. "She smells like Cari."

I hadn't noticed Cari's smell before. Not since the night I'd gotten a whiff of Marechal. She smells strong, succulent, and yes, sweet. There is adrenaline coursing through her veins. Her sweet blood is primed for my bite, and mine alone.

I snarl at my brother, my lip curling up as I flash my fangs. The message is clear: I will not be sharing.

Viri holds up his hands. "Fine, don't share. But keep your hands off my stash of bags in the fridge."

I wait until he is out the door before I relax my shoulders. I prepare myself to answer Marechal's questions about Viri and his strangeness. It's always hard to explain away my brother's oddness.

I had once thought that our Domitia had scarred Hadrian the most. I realized soon after we thought she was dead that I was wrong. Hadrian has recovered. I fear Viri never will.

When I turn to Marechal, she is not looking after Virius. She is glaring at me. The determined set to her chin is back.

"I am done playing around with you, Gaius Serrano. You are going to tell me where my sister is. And you're going to tell me what you are about, buying up the controlling shares to Durand Vineyard."

I am caught off guard. It is a rare feat. That is not at all what I was expecting her to say.

"My patience is wearing thin," she says.

The woman is magnificent. She might've given Domitia a run for her money. As soon as the thought arises, I bury it. I don't want that demon anywhere near this avenging angel.

"Aren't you a bossy little thing," I say.

I itch to take her over my lap and spank some obedience into her. As I advance on her, she takes two strong strides towards me, closing the distance. Her wine-colored eyes are tequila bright. Another man would've backed down. Instead, my dick punches the front of my pants, eager to breach the rest of the distance between us.

"Don't call me bossy," she growls, though it's more like the purr of an irate kitten. "Whenever a woman corrects a man or speaks her mind, she's called bossy by that man. Likely because her words shriveled up his manhood."

"Trust me, *minou*. My manhood is anything but shriveled."

Marechal's gaze dips low, to my pants. The evidence is stark for her to see. I watch her throat work as she takes me in. My tongue traces over my incisors. Hunger rushes through me, down past my stomach and into my loins.

I know then that I'm going to have this woman. I'm going to have her repeatedly. I'm going to have her thoroughly. And she will be begging.

"You're a bastard, you know that?"

I do know that. But it's for entirely different reasons than she could ever fathom.

"You've taken my sister," she continues. "And now my business."

"*Minou*, I haven't touched your *business*. You'll be screaming my name when I do."

"I would've fixed it."

There's a break in her voice that makes me stop and pay attention. The stern look on her face changes, and some of the strength leaves her. I have the urge to prop her up. I don't like Marechal Durand weakened and broken. Not unless it's by my hand.

"I raised Cari all by myself after our mother died. And you and your brother have just taken her from me."

"Cari and Hadrian are just on their honeymoon. They will return." Reassuring a woman is not my strong suit, and I'm not sure I'm doing a fair job of it here.

"I've been running the day to day of my family's wine business since I was fifteen. I brought it back from the brink while my father grieved our mother. I would've brought it back again. But you've taken that from me."

Now I am clueless as to what we are talking about. That happens often with me when I'm engaged in a conversation with a woman that has nothing to do with sex.

"Don't act innocent," Marechal hisses.

"I'm anything but innocent. But I don't have any idea what you mean about your business. What is happening? Are you in some kind of trouble?"

"I've never needed a man to come in and save me. I'm no damsel."

No, Marechal Durand definitely isn't the passive princess type. She is a warrior. A woman it would take a calculated assault to break down. I much prefer that type of strength to a female in distress.

"I would've covered the debts. I would've brought Durand back. I would've handled it all."

"I don't doubt it," I say.

Marechal blinks at me as though she doesn't believe my words. It would appear this strong woman has the weight of the world on her shoulders —at least the weight of acres of a vineyard, and a family that doesn't seem to appreciate her load.

I reach my hand out. Her breath catches on my thumb as I tilt her chin up. I lift her proud head until her eyes are gazing directly into mine. I know now that I'll need to tug a little harder to bend her to my will.

"Come, Marechal," I command.

Her lips part. I get a sneak peek at the rosé of the flesh there. Her full lips are plumper than a grape. I content myself with the knowledge that I'll soon be sinking my teeth into them.

"Come now, it's time to rest."

Marechal's lids droop, hiding the ripe plum of her dark irises. In another second, she is in my arms. I lift her form with ease as I walk out of the cellar.

"Don't worry, *minou*. I'll take care of everything."

8

G*aius*

"WHERE IS SHE? Is she still here? Is she hurt? Did I hurt her?"

I stand in the doorway as I watch Hadrian pull his bride close. Cari's fangs are out and dripping even as her gaze is troubled. The bruising on her upper arms where Hadrian must have held her back is fast fading. There are rips in her sundress, exposing the chest of her honeyed skin, skin so much like her sister's. Though my fangs don't ache at the sight of my new sister-in-law's bared flesh.

"It's all right," Hadrian soothes, tucking Cari under his chin. There are scratches on his face and forearms, no doubt delivered by his newly-turned bride. His bruises are fading even faster than Cari's, the struggle of a moment ago forgotten. "You didn't get anywhere near her."

Cari buries her head at Hadrian's heart. Just days ago, Hadrian clawed at his chest to feed a dying Cari the lifeblood from his heart. It's the best way to turn a new vampire. It was the first and only time any of my brothers have done it.

We all watched Domitia turn young boys, countless times. We never discussed it out loud, but silently we had all sworn never to make another of our kind. But that was because we'd only seen it done to enslave or gain power. We'd never seen it done for love.

There is a pang in my chest as I watch the two of them together. I don't understand the feeling. I've watched Hadrian with Domitia many times. Our sire enjoyed having the two of us inside her at the same time.

I do not miss those ménages, mainly because the sexual escapades broke Hadrian a little each time she forced him into them. Which, of course, was why Domitia insisted on them. The demoness couldn't get off if there wasn't pain involved: preferably another's pain.

So no, I feel no love for my sire. More than anything, I want her out of my nightmares so whatever tightness I feel in my chest isn't from thoughts of her.

"I can't believe I almost attacked my own sister," Cari whimpers. "I smelled her blood and I couldn't stop myself. If you hadn't been there…"

"Shhh," Hadrian hushes her. "Gaius sent her off the property. She's safe and sound."

"She's not gone," I say, pouring myself a glass of blood-tinged wine. "She's in my bed."

Hadrian and Cari turn blazing eyes on me. Cari's fangs elongate once more as her eyes dart frantically around the dining room. Hadrian's fists clench as he glares at me.

"I put her down for a nap."

"Why would you do that?" demands Hadrian.

Why indeed? We have a few workers on the vineyard, shifters we use to work for us during the daylight hours. One of them could've driven Marechal home. But the thought of someone else touching her, the thought of her being beyond my grasp, made those same muscles clench in my chest.

"You know Cari is in a fragile state. Why would you keep her sister here?"

"I don't know, brother." I down the glass of sanguine wine; the iron and alcohol go straight to my head. "Why did you buy the Durand vineyard debts?"

Hadrian's fingers unclench. He jerks his head away from me, but not before I hear the curse under his breath.

"You what?" Cari's fangs flash again. "Hadrian, is this true? Did you do some sort of hostile takeover of my family's business?"

Hadrian takes a deep breath. He sinks his fang into his lower lip, as though he is mulling over the right words to say. Having known the man for centuries, I know that he is carefully crafting a lie. Having known the man for just a couple of weeks, it would appear his new bride is wise to his ways, as well.

"You asshole," Cari hisses. "You can boss me around in the bedroom. But if you want to try it in any other room, especially when it comes to my family, you're gonna get a rude surprise. Especially once my sister wakes up."

I chuckle at that. I've been on the receiving end of Marechal Durand, the boss businesswoman. I know a weaker man would've cowered. That iron maiden attitude only serves to make my dick hard. I wanted to bend her over her office desk and lick her from her toes to her clit.

"The vineyard was drowning in debt," says Hadrian. "Lucius Frangelico was about to purchase it."

I wasn't aware of either of those two details. We have made peace with the vampire king, but I don't want him sniffing anywhere near Marechal. I move from my post on the wall, coming to stand at Hadrian's side.

"Marechal's going to lose her shit when she finds out," says Cari.

"She already has," I say. "That's what she was doing here."

Now it's Cari who cringes. "Did she bite your head off?"

"She tried." I grin. "Luckily, she's not the one with fangs."

Cari flashes me her fangs with a toothy grin. Her features are so like Marechal's that the vision of a tight-bunned, stern-faced vampiress glaring down at me makes my dick weep with want.

"Hadrian, you shouldn't have gotten into my family's business without consulting me," says Cari.

"I know the vineyard was in some trouble, but you should've let Marechal handle it. Marechal always handles it."

Something about that statement irks me. I think back to Marechal's relaxed posture as she'd lain with her foot bound in a knot of rope. And then again when she'd come face to face with the suspension toys in the dungeon. For a woman who always handles everything, Marechal Durand desperately needs someone to take her in hand.

"You're already on her bastard list for running off and marrying me," Cari says. "Now you've taken her business from her. You are not going to win brother-in-law of the year anytime this decade."

"Luckily, we have a lifetime," says Hadrian.

"But what are we going to do today?" Cari says. "She definitely hates you now."

"I'll handle it," I say.

"You?" says Hadrian. "She already doesn't like you."

I scoff at that. But then Cari nods in agreement.

"Well, you are exactly the kind of man she dislikes," says Cari.

"Charming, well dressed, cultured?"

"A ladies' man who is now her boss," says Cari. "Just know that if you try to change anything about the business she's run for over a decade, she will make your life miserable."

"Why would I change anything? Your sister is brilliant at what she does."

I've been keeping track of the Durand Vineyards for decades now. Their signature wine is an elegant nod to the classic vintages. Though I'm not one for blends and hybrids, I can't deny the innovations their vintners are making. This past week, I learned that the head vintner is Marechal.

"Yeah, she's brilliant, and she knows it." Cari smiles proudly, her hunger all but forgotten. Then those Chianti-colored eyes of hers sparkle. "Hey, if you two get together, you can turn her and we can all be one big happy family."

My mouth goes slack. I might want to fuck Cari's sister, but I don't do relationships or monogamy. Hell, I am rarely willing to commit enough to actually stick my cock in a woman's cunt. Down her throat? Sure, if she behaves. Between her tits? Yeah, if she's lucky.

But I'm not about to tell Cari that. Luckily, my brother comes to my aid.

"That's not going to happen," says Hadrian. "Gaius never wears the same socks twice, much less keeps the same woman."

I want to protest. That isn't entirely true. I've been playing at the club most nights this past week, and came home wearing yesterday's socks at least twice.

"We've talked about this," Hadrian goes on. "If Marechal finds out what you've become, we'll need to wipe her mind, like we did your brother. That didn't go so well."

Arneis Durand was in the same accident that had nearly cost Cari her life. Hadrian saved him by giving him a taste of his healing blood. Then I wiped the man's mind.

I don't want to tamper with Marechal's mind. I like the fight in her. What I want is her submission. Now that I am her boss, I could have a taste of it.

9

———

Marechal

I'M NOT USUALLY a good sleeper. Dreams are always thin wisps to me. When I wake, I can never truly hold on to what I'd been dreaming about.

Not so this time.

I feel each braid of the rope against my ankles. The twines loop around my thighs, curling up over my torso and binding my hands to the Saint Andrew's Cross at the center of the wine cellar. I hear the whisper of the flogger's tresses as they are dragged on the floor. Each hum of the tails sends a shiver along my thighs that urges me to clench my ass.

But I can't move. I am bound, held still, and awaiting his command.

The sound of his footfalls is a booming drumbeat in my ears as he steps onto the scene. His presence mutes the light of the glowing candles. Each flame leans towards him, drawn as though the wicks are the moths and he is fire.

His jet black hair falls across his forehead, shading his dark gaze from me. His tongue snakes out of his mouth and licks at his lower lip. Again, I feel the need to clench. But this time it isn't my ass that needs to grip at something.

The channel between my legs is desperate for something to fill it. It's a feeling that is foreign to me. I lost my virginity in high school. I can't even remember the boy's last name, or his face. It wasn't memorable. Nor were any of the few times I had sex after that.

Sex was simply a chore that came with having a boyfriend. When I realized that having a boyfriend didn't serve my bottom line, I stopped the practice, and saw that I had no need for sex. It had never been memorable, anyway.

But watching Gaius handle a flogger while I'm

strapped and bound to a cross makes my lady bits sit up and pay attention. Even in a dream.

As I'd felt when I was caught by the rope and he'd loomed over me, there is a weightlessness that settles over my captive shoulders. I feel free, even though I can't escape. I can't remember a single worry from my life.

More than anything, I want to stay asleep, in this dream. The relief of hanging here, waiting for Gaius to make a move, is heaven.

He lifts his gaze to my face. My back arches off the cross, my breasts strain to him, the nipples going harder than pebbles.

His hand rises. The tails of the flogger murmur with a hum of excitement as the twirls shift in his hand.

I need to press my thighs together but know that I will get no relief. I know that only his hands wielding that device will be the thing that does it. Which is strange. I have never had an orgasm before. I doubt any woman has ever had one. It's a farce made up by the porn industry. If Meg Ryan can fake one on cue then it can't be real.

Still, it is nice to dream. It is nice to be aroused. It is nice to explore my secret fantasies in the comfort of my depraved mind. I have never let my curiosity about the world of BDSM be known to anyone.

Well, except for one boyfriend. But when he'd tried to comply with my wishes and given me a light, chuckling swat on the butt, I dumped him the next day and never spoke of it again.

Back in the wine cellar that was actually a sex dungeon, Gaius Serrano looked like he knew exactly how to use a flogger. He probably knew how to tie a woman to a cross, since he'd been so adept at unraveling me from the knot earlier.

But this will only ever be a dream. A dream I can't afford to keep having. There is too much work to do, and I have to get up and do it.

The moment I open my eyes, all the pressures slam back into me. My hands aren't bound, they are free to pick up the mantle left to me by my parents. My feet aren't restricted, they can carry the load on my shoulders and get my family out of this latest mess.

I know there are bills to deal with, a payroll total that I can't meet, berries that need looking after, equipment that needs fixing, a brother who is unwell, a sister to find, and now an Italian family to wrestle my business back from.

Is Gaius Italian? I've caught a lilting French

accent every now and again. He certainly doesn't know French well. The word for kitten is *minette*. So why does he keep calling me *minou*?

Italian, French, or whatever, I'll deal with him... Just as soon as I figure out where I am.

It takes a moment for my eyes to adjust to the darkness. The first thing I notice is that I am not in my bed. I'm not in my room. The sheets I'm lying on are softer than a newly sprung grape leaf. I'm in a four-poster bed that looks like it grew from the roots of a tree. It smells of old oak and fresh earth.

Not a single light is on in the room. It is lit by candles, and the wicks all lean towards one corner of the room. I know instinctively who is looming in the shadows.

"Mr. Serrano?"

I sit up in the bed, thankful that I am still clothed. The only thing that has been taken from me are my shoes. I see them sitting on the side table.

"What am I doing here?" I demand.

"You fell ill." His voice is like honeyed wine: sweet on the way down, but the burn comes later in the throat. "I brought you inside to rest."

That doesn't sound like me. I've never taken ill a day in my life. I've been far too busy.

"You've been working yourself to the bone, Ms.

Durand," he says. "There's no longer a need for that."

"And so it begins? Now that you've purchased my family's business, you think you'll tell me what to do?"

Gaius's grin spreads as he separates himself from the shadows. The flames catch on a flash of white teeth. My heartbeat kicks up. I feel like prey that's been cornered, and am now being played with before the eating begins.

"I've spoken with Hadrian. He purchased the vineyard's debts as a wedding present to Cari. He has no interest in running the business or interfering in any way."

That should be good news. But the fist around my heart does not loosen. Instead, I feel more stress pressing down on my shoulders.

"When it comes to winemaking, Ms. Durand, I know that you are the best. I would not deign to tell you how to run your vineyard."

He takes a step towards me. The sound of his heel impacting the hardwood of the floor is the same drumbeat from my dream.

"In your labs, you will maintain complete control," he continues.

Another step closer. My heartbeat kicks up.

Again, I feel as though this man is a beast prowling towards me. But me, being me, I do not back down.

"You will have control over your staff and the finances. I assume it was your father and brother who mismanaged funds?"

I do not answer. My father is blameless in my eyes. He'd lost the woman he'd loved. He was never quite right after my mother died. I did what I could to keep us afloat. I was so busy with the day to day that I did not notice we were drowning.

I am so busy in my reverie that I failed to notice that Gaius has come upon me. He rests a hand on my bare calf. I shudder at the contact. I look down to see that he is focusing on the markings on my leg, left by the rope. Though I do not have pale skin, my flesh bruises easily. That mark won't fade until tomorrow.

"You are in complete control, *minou.* I am only here to offer you a hand where you may need it."

His voice is hypnotic. If I were a weaker woman, I'd be under his spell. But I am me, so I cock my head to the side and give him a pitying look.

"I don't need your hand. What I need is the controlling interest in my company back."

Once again, a slow grin spreads across his handsome face. I can't take my eyes off his lips as they stretch from plump and biteable to thin and wicked. Kissing was the only thing I'd enjoyed in my dating life.

That, and being held. But none of my partners had had the strong, thick arms of Gaius Serrano. I bet he could hold me tight. Carry me, even. But that's something I'll never know. I'll never allow myself to get close enough to him to find out. That wicked grin might be dangerous to some women; it is lost on me.

"Name your price," I say.

His brows lift. The move is a challenge. I have no idea what he's about to say, what price he'll name. But whatever it is, I'm willing to pay it to get my family's company back.

"My price is an orgasm."

I blink slowly. But as my lids lower, I realize the mistake in that. It would be dangerous to have this man out of my sight even for the blink of an eye.

"I beg your pardon?" I say.

"My price. It's an orgasm."

10

G*aius*

"You're a pig."

That's Marechal's response once she finds her voice again. I note that it is not a *no*. I also note that her nostrils flare, her breath quickens, and her thighs press together. That is all the answer I need to press forward.

"You do know that pigs are used to find truffles," I say, "those rare, delicious treats."

Marechal sits at the top of the mattress. I remain at the bottom of the bed. My hand is stretched across the sea of memory foam between us. My fingers still graze her calf, feeling the indentations left by the ropes.

The fact that she hasn't yanked her leg away also tells me what I need to know about her true desires. Marechal Durand might be in charge in the business world, but in the bedroom, she is completely out of touch with her needs.

"You do know that a truffle hog can't actually eat the fruit it unearths," she says.

I throw back my head and laugh at this. She is a delight. It's been a long time since I've had to work for it. I'm going to enjoy the hell out of making this woman submit to me.

She finally notices my hand on her leg. She pulls her calf away, tucking it under her but not rising from the bed. Confusion and anger mar her face. Clearly, her mind knows she should flee, but her body wants to stay.

"You once said that there was no such thing as an orgasm," I say while maintaining my distance from her on the bed.

"It's a scientific fact based on many research studies." Marechal's tone is once again haughty, and no longer breathless. She rises from the mattress and collects her shoes, sliding one heel on at a time.

"Ninety-five percent of men experience a pleasurable spasm of the loins, whereas less than twenty-five percent of women report experiencing any such release during intercourse. You simply can't argue with science, Mr. Serrano."

"Not going to argue, Ms. Durand. I simply would like to try an alternative method to see if we can arrive at a different result."

"I am not having sex with you to take back my family business." She stands proud in the center of my bedroom. With her heels back on, it's as though she's regained her superpower. Her shoulders are back, her head is high. Her hands are even on her hips in the akimbo pose of a superhero. She is Wonder Woman in a business skirt, no cape needed.

"I would never make you do anything against your will," I say, leaning back against the bedpost, allowing my gaze to take her in.

She smirks as though there's no way that I could make her do anything she didn't want to. Little does she know. It would be better for her if I had no interest in making her crawl to me. Now that I have that image in my mind, I know I will edge this woman mercilessly, bringing her to the brink of pleasure and then pulling her back. Over and over again I'll push her, until her back arches off the bed and she lands in a puddle of bliss at my feet.

Some protective instinct inside her must see my intentions because she takes a step back.

"I don't want to fuck you," I say, as I rise from the bed.

She hesitates. Uncertainty is clear in her dark, plum eyes. She winces. Was that perhaps a ding to her feminine pride?

"But your money is no good with me, either."

"So what exactly do you want?"

"Your pleasure. Give me five minutes of your time. If I can't bring you to experience this elusive idea known as the female release, then I'll hand over half of the Durand shares my family just purchased."

Her eyes flash. I can't tell if it's from the possibility of receiving pleasure, or the potential for getting half the shares back. My bet would be on the latter.

"Five minutes." I hold up my hand, fingers splayed. "I keep my pants on. You keep your skirt on."

"Then how will you..." She waves her hand between us, her honey-gold cheeks flushing to amber.

"You let me worry about that, *minou*."

Her fingers curl into a fist. She is considering it. Not that I doubted she would.

"Why do you want this?" she asks.

I decide on the truth. "You're a strong woman, Marechal. Smart—brilliant, actually. Capable. I simply want your attention."

"You had my attention when you instituted a hostile takeover of my life's work."

"I'll give it back if I can't bring you pleasure. What do you have to lose?"

"What do you get if you can... do it?"

"If I can do it then you'll let me do it again."

Marechal tugs at her bottom lip as she's thinking this over. I know it's already a done deal. I can scent her arousal. She needs this, and by the Fates, I want to be the man to give it to her. Again, and then again. So much so that my patience is starting to wane.

As the seconds tick by, I fight to hold myself very still. I want to throw her back on the bed, strap her down, and take her clit between my teeth. There would be nothing she could do about it. And I know without a doubt that I would bring her pleasure enough to make her forget anything but my name.

"How long did you say?"

The beast inside of me stirs. I have to swallow

down my eagerness to have this woman. I also struggle to keep to the original time. "Five minutes."

Marechal takes a deep breath. Slowly, her hands slide down her skirt, evening out nonexistent wrinkles. Her heels clack as she walks to the bed and takes a seat.

I uncuff my shirt and roll up my sleeve. With my forearm bare, I turn my wrist until the face of my Rolex is visible to both of us. With sure fingers, I set the timer.

11

M _arechal_

Is this what a prostitute feels like? At least they would receive a cash benefit for their troubles. There is no guarantee that I will reap the reward I'm willing to give up my virtue for.

I've already given up so much for my family and this business. What's this one more thing? It's not like I actually believe in the female orgasm. I can lie on my back while he fumbles around in my lady bits. It'll basically be like a visit to the OBGYN. If it takes playing doctor with an infantile, grown man to win back what I've worked so hard for all my life, it will be worth it. I'll just have to lie back and think of the vineyard.

The workday is over, but there's still a ton to do when I get back home. That's a casualty of sleeping where you work. I try to recall the mountain of paperwork I have to go through when I get back. There will be bills, invoices, and sales reports, not to mention added payroll now that the nighttime harvest is underway.

Though each time I try to mentally call up a task and add it to the list, the thought goes hazy. My attention wanders, meandering down long, curved lines of fresh vines until I am back here. In this room. With this man.

Gaius hasn't touched me. He hasn't touched himself, either, the possibility of which had been another of my concerns. He simply gazes at me.

What? Does he think he can make me spontaneously combust with just that smoldering glance? The asshole. He probably does think that.

So why do I feel my nipples going hard as he looks down my body? Why do my thighs press together as he cocks his head to peer down? My heels click together like I'm Dorothy, ready to fly home from Oz. The clicking sound reminds me that I'm doing this so that I can get my home back.

Tick, tick, tick. The only other sound in the room is that of Gaius's watch. He's wasted at least thirty seconds in this staring contest. He's got less than four and a half minutes left.

The bed shakes as he steps closer to me. He hasn't taken a seat on the mattress. He's still standing. I realize the reason the bed is shaking is because of me.

I have no idea what is happening to me. I must be out of my mind. My brain is only clear when I look at him. My body tingles and tightens with just a glance from him. And now my limbs are trembling, and he hasn't even touched me.

And then he does.

Surprisingly, I don't jump when his fingertips graze my calf. He touches the center of my right shin, the part where it is more bone than flesh. I shaved last night but I'm so sensitive that I can feel the millimeter's worth of growth itching for more of his touch.

His touch is pleasant, but definitely not enough to delude me into a real or imagined inner muscle spasm. I say nothing to dissuade or encourage Gaius.

Time is ticking as he moves slowly. Right now, the second's hand is on my side.

Gaius's index finger dips behind my knee. My leg jerks straight on the mattress. The movement causes my back to arch. A low cauldron of heat is starting to burn at the base of my spine. A hum of sensation slowly radiates outward, encircling my hips.

My eyes are half-lidded. I wrench them open wide to see that his gaze is on my face, not on what he's doing. In the dim light of the room, his smirk is muted. He smiles faintly, just a curl at the left corner of his mouth.

Why isn't he trying to look up my skirt? Why is he so focused on my face? His gaze darts from my eyes to my mouth. He even takes one of his precious seconds to glance at my nose.

My nostrils flare under his perusal. In an effort to lower the flagging flesh there, I swallow, only to have to swallow again, and then again. My mouth is watering as his fingers trace a slow path to my inner thigh.

It's no longer just the pointed beacon of his index finger. The thick pad of his thumb draws lazy circles on my flesh as the long length of his middle finger leads the charge.

Onward. Upward. His hands climb.

My lower back continues to arch off the mattress. No matter how deeply I breathe, it won't relax back down. That cauldron of warmth in my hips has burned a path around to the front of me and is stoking embers there.

What is happening? Is it possible? Am I going to lose this wager?

Without any preamble or warning, Gaius pulls his hand away. Not entirely. He rests the full weight of his palm on my inner thigh. If he stretched out his long fingers, he would brush the edges of my sex. Instead of reaching out, he bends down.

I prepare myself to recoil from his advance. But he comes no closer to me. He simply goes down to his knees. On the floor. Not the bed.

The way he's arranged his form puts him on eye level with me. Still, somehow, it feels as though he continues to loom over me. He kneels on the floor as though he's praying for me. Or mourning me at my sickbed. Both images have validity.

A few seconds ago, I was ready to call out for a lord and savior over what this man was making me feel. Just the thought of it must mean I'm mentally disturbed, and might benefit from some time in the looney bin.

There are two minutes left on the clock.

Less than a moment ago, I thought he just might be able to introduce me to some form of pleasure in the sexual act. Now, with less than half the time left, I know I'm about to win this bet. As soon as I think the thought, my hips jackknife off the bed.

"*S'intaller, minou.*"

Settle down? How can I settle down with his fingers tracing the lining of my thong? His touch is light but it is eliciting a reaction that I am not in control of.

I don't know if I'm unsettled by the intimate touch of his fingers, or the out of control jerking of my limbs. I'm not a woman prone to be anything but in control. I don't know how to react. I don't know how to think.

Apparently, I'm not thinking. My mind is empty of anything except sparks of pleasure. My breasts ache. My belly is trembling. There is a pressure building at the core of me.

And then he stops.

His hand is still under my skirt. Looking down, I can see the outline of his knuckles beneath the fabric. They are less than an inch away from where I want him to be, where I know I need him to be. I want to scream in frustration, but I don't dare give him the satisfaction.

Plus, I need to win. He has less than a minute left in this game he's playing. It's a game he has no hope of winning. But I'm starting to wonder if that was his aim.

When he touches me again, his index and middle finger land on the plumpest part of my thong. The area is soaking wet, and for a moment, I worry I've embarrassed myself. That area has only ever been this wet when I've gone to the bathroom. But my bladder is empty. All that moisture came from somewhere else inside me.

With a flick of his thumb, Gaius rubs at the crest of my sex. The skin there is engorged. It throbs under his touch, instantly soaking the top part of my underwear. My mind blanks as that cauldron inside of me blazes ever higher.

The wetness pouring out of my sex is like gasoline. It covers my entire mons. It spills into the cracks between my sex and my thighs. One more flick of his fingers and the match will ignite, burning me alive in a blaze of pleasure.

I hold my breath, preparing to be pulled under its heat, to be buried alive in the flames. I can already hear the fire truck's alarm blaring its warning.

But no. That's not an emergency vehicle. It is the alarm clock.

Time is up.

Gaius pulls his hand from beneath my skirt and sits back on his haunches. "Ah, Ms. Durand, it looks as though I've lost."

He doesn't sound contrite. He doesn't sound sorry. He looks at me with that same smile as when he made this deal: patient, predatory, waiting to pounce. He's taken a chunk out of me, and I didn't realize it until it was too late.

12

G*aius*

I BRING my hand to my mouth as we eye each other. Slowly, I extend my index finger and take a languid lick. I just barely keep myself from moaning. I've eaten a lot of cunny in my many centuries. They are much like the different taste profiles of wine.

Some women have firm, bitter cunts, like a glass of red. They are best served warm, after riding a sex toy or the tails of my flogger for a long time.

Then there are the females with the crisp, tart

taste of white wine. Best to finger fuck their G-spots hard and repeatedly to increase the zest in their juices.

Women who tend to blush frequently fall somewhere in the middle, like a rosé. They are perfect for a quick snack, as it doesn't take much to get them off and get the essence flowing.

Marechal is none of the above. She is like an aged port or sherry, a sweet dessert wine that's so light and airy that before you realize it, you've downed the glass. When you go to stand, you stumble and see that you've gone punch drunk.

I stand now, carefully putting my feet under me. I can't let her see how much she's affected me. That would ruin the game I'm playing with her.

Her body still trembles from the release I denied her. Her dark eyes are saucers of disbelief. I'm moderately surprised her nipples haven't sliced through the silk of her blouse.

I've only tasted a few vintages such as her. Those women, I kept around for some time. I know then, as I flick my tongue under my fingernail, that I will be going back for more. And the next time it will be for a direct hit of her juices.

It's rare that I drink from the same pussy more than once. Why bother, when humans and shifters are so plentiful and at the ready? In the last few decades, I haven't sipped from the same neck or femoral artery twice.

I haven't fucked a woman in that long either.

Oh, I've had them suck me off. But the thought of getting lost in a woman's body is anathema to me —likely because the last woman I properly fucked liked to dig her claws into my balls and watch them bleed. Even with Domitia gone, I preferred to keep my dick to myself unless I was shoving it deep down a submissive's throat.

On the bed, Marechal parts her lips. My dick stands to attention, wanting into that orifice. *S'installer*, I tell it. We will both have what we want soon. Likely within the next five minutes.

"I trust the shares will be transferred over into my name by the opening of business tomorrow?" Her tone is clipped, businesslike once more.

Marechal sits up, surprisingly elegant even though I've rucked up her skirt. She carefully places both feet on the ground. The stems of her heels knock against the floor, but the sound is not an invitation to come inside.

"Of course," I say, matching her professional tone.

She nods. Her shoulders are erect, back straight,

head high. But she won't meet my eyes. Somehow she's looking down her nose at me without looking directly at me. Her haughty attitude only serves to want me to make her beg even harder.

"I'll have the paperwork drawn up tonight," I say, straightening out my shirt and refastening my cuff. "You'll have forty-five percent ownership of your company."

Her gaze flashes to mine in the light of that math. There's a tick in her jaw. I can hear her molars grind. There is a tremble in her pinky finger—a slight one, but it's there. Any other woman would be on her knees, thighs parted, palms up, waiting for my command. Not this one.

Marechal Durand is the strongest woman I've met in a lifetime. I crave to see her back bend, to break that iron will of hers until her pussy is putty in the palm of my hands. Working Marechal Durand up is fast becoming my new favorite pastime. I'm sure the pleasure will only be surpassed by working her over.

"For now." The two words are clipped. "Thank you for your time, Mr. Serrano. I'll be going home now."

Her heels are the sounds of war drums as they impact the floor. My ears twitch as they catch a hint of the slickness on her inner thighs. If not for those thick stems on her vintage shoes, Marechal would be sliding across the floor.

She moves quickly past me, giving me a delectable view of her backside. Fuck, if I can't wait to bend her over my knee. But she's almost out the door.

"Wait!"

Her heels come to a screeching halt. They've probably left a mark on my pristine floor. Marechal turns, giving me a wary glare. Damn, can the woman arch an eyebrow.

"What?" Her tone could cut glass. The cool breeze rolling off her shoulders does nothing to dampen my hard-on.

"You promised to look at my vines."

Her gaze dips to my crotch. There's no problem with that particular vine. It is hard and eager for her attention. Very soon, I'll place it on her tongue for her to suckle.

She parts those lush lips in what I know will be a refusal. But before she can utter a word, I hold out my hands, arms outstretched, as though to show there is nothing up my sleeves.

"Just because I lost our friendly wager..." I begin.

Both her brows go sky high at that. I hold up my

palms to show they are empty, even though I can still scent her sweet smell on my fingers.

"I didn't think you'd hold your winning and my failing over my head."

Now her mouth gapes open, but only for a second before she slams it shut. That dark plum gaze narrows on me with suspicion. Fates, when's the last time I've had such an intelligent, discerning woman?

"I would appreciate you taking a look at my vine, as a professional courtesy," I say. "Surely you can give me another moment of your time."

The breath she lets out is low and shaky. Can she sense I threw that bet? Does she recognize that I had her in the palm of my hand, literally? It's been so long since I've played a game of catch and release. Usually, women throw themselves at me for the release they know I can give.

"I'll grab a sample on my way out," she says.

It's not what I wanted. But this is the pattern with her. I incline my head to her. She turns on her heel and makes a dash for the door. I let her go.

Let her think to herself that she isn't already on my hook. Her gait isn't the confident stride it usually is. Her pussy is aching for me, aching for release. Soon enough, I'll catch her. Then I'll dangle her on the line until she begs for mercy.

I'll just have to keep our tryst from Cari, which in turn means keeping it from Hadrian. Despite the pretty family picture my new sister-in-law painted earlier, I don't do relationships. Marechal is going to be a lovely distraction. But only for a few days.

13

M*arechal*

THERE IS no distinction between dreaming and waking. My body hums from a fitful rest to an energized alertness. Like a vine greeting the new day's sun, I unfurl my arms and stretch my limbs. As I stretch the length of my body, I don't hear the usual snap, crackle, and pop of tired tendons. Where I do feel the weight is in my core.

A tingle persists between my thighs. A throb of need that I have never experienced before. Because I'd never known what I'd been missing.

Last night, Gaius Serrano brought me out from under a deep, dark cave. He brought me down a long, dim hallway with lights on either wall flaring to life with each of his guiding steps. At the end of the corridor, I spied the first ray of sunlight. The rays reached out to me, beckoning me to me with their warmth. I hadn't even known I was cold until that moment. Before I could touch the glass panes of the window, Gaius pulled the curtains closed.

This morning, daylight streams into my open curtains. The full force of the sun's light captures my face. I'm still burrowed under the comforter. Yet somehow, I am left cold. When I press my thighs together, the ache there persists.

Last night wasn't the first time a man put his hands down my panties. Back in high school, Wally O'Neal's efforts had been pointless and embarrassing. Or, rather, pointed and uncomfortable. The man's fingernails had been longer than mine. He was a much better Dungeon Master and aspiring wand wielder than he was a lover.

Sex hadn't interested me much after that. I'd had sex with my college boyfriend, Jordan Riley. He wasn't a college student, though. He was my professor, one of the world's foremost oenologists. The man was brilliant when it came to the study of ancient wines. I could listen to him wax philosophical for hours about the fermentation of rice in Predynastic China. His theories would be all I thought about during his two-minute pumping action between my legs. After he rolled over and fell asleep, I'd pull my panties back on and get my kicks reading his research notes.

When Gaius put his fingers on me, my mind blanked into a pure blackness of bliss, punctuated by tiny starbursts of light that promised a big explosion.

Would he want to do it again? That is a stupid question. I know he would. Handsome, rich men like to play power games. The real question is: would I let him play me?

As of now, I have forty-five percent of my family's company back in my grasp. Gaius still holds the controlling amount. What would I have to let him do to me to get another six percent?

A sheen of sweat coats my forehead at the thought. I jerk the covers off me. My bare feet crash down onto the cold floor, shocking some sense back into me.

That was a one-time event. I've spent all my life having to prove my intelligence and capability in a man's world. I will use my head to get the rest of the shares back.

With a purposeful inhale, I push myself up off the bed. I go through my morning necessaries and then get dressed.

I pull on a bra, but the silky lace feels too rough on my breasts. The matching panty set feels tight at my thighs; the material brushes against my swollen core, and I ache. I pull on a tight skirt, hoping it will help keep me together. All it does is make me feel confined, make me feel the need to step out of it. Instead, I slip on a pair of six-inch heels—entirely impractical for the walk I have to do in the field today, but the shoes make me feel powerful.

I leave my room and head for my lab. Stepping up to the open window there, I can see the entire vineyard. The sight of even rows of green that stretch on for miles settles something in me. Staring at the uniformity is what finally cools the ache between my legs. My shoulders straighten. My tits lift, but not because of any man. It's because of all that I have built.

With the yield of this season's harvest, I know I'll have enough to buy back the last six shares to retake control of my business. Gaius said he wasn't interested in my money, but I'm willing to offer the entire profit if it'll put me back in control of my destiny.

On my desk is a wilting vine. The color of the leaves is not any of the Durand's signature berries. Nor are they one of my hybrid blends.

Then I remember; this is the vine I took from the Serrano vineyard before I left. At the roots are the telltale white spots to indicate rot. But there's more.

The green leaves are discolored with splotches of red. In some places, there are raised pockmarks along the veins. I place the specimen under a microscope to get a better look. What I see there doesn't make sense.

Grapevines are tough plants. They can survive cold winter storms, an invasion of pests and, in some cases, flooding. The Serrano vine looks like it's been through each of these catastrophes all at once—when not a single one of those instances has happened in this valley.

A light tap on the exterior door brings my head up. Zahara stands in the open door. Her gaze is cast down as she waits for me to acknowledge her. Before I do, I glance up at the clock. It's well after lunchtime. I'm shocked to see that I've been examining this vine for hours.

"Yes, Zahara, please come in."

She shuffles into my lab. As she nears my desk, her hand rises. I take the slip of paper she offers. On the document, I see her carefully written script detailing the date, hours worked last night, and the number of workers. It's a larger number of people than I expected.

"We're not trying to cheat you, Ms. Durand."

"I didn't think you were."

"Times are hard back home," she says. "Jobs are scarce. That's why there are more of us this year."

Zahara's blouse slips off her shoulder, revealing brown skin and a red, raised pockmark. The bruise looks similar to the disease on the plants, but in a straight line and close together. Like the swipe of fingernails.

"Are you okay, Zahara?"

Her gaze lifts to meet mine. She blinks as she searches my face. Whatever she's looking for, she doesn't find it, because she pulls up the loose fabric to cover the mark.

"I'm ready to work," she says. "With more of my cousins here, we should get the harvest done in half the time."

It's clear she's not willing to talk to me about her bruise. I have a mind to fire all of the new males she's brought with her, starting with the misogynist from yesterday. Instead, I unlock the safe where I keep the cash for the day workers. I hand her the money noted on the invoice. Then I tug a few more bills loose, slipping them into her blouse where I saw the wound.

I realize too late that the move, even between two women, might have crossed a line. But Zahara doesn't flinch. She holds my gaze as she retrieves the money I stuffed down her shirt and hands it back to me.

"I don't do handouts, Ms. Durand."

Color stains my cheeks. I want to tell her that's not what that was. I don't want to give her a hand. I want to give her the ability to run if she needs to.

"It's not for your hands," I say. "It's for your feet, in case you need to get away."

The same small smile from yesterday plays on her lips. "History tells me never to take a gift from a colonizer."

"My family wasn't part of that. I'm second-generation French-American."

Zahara nods, but she still doesn't take the money. Her gaze is on the vine on the table. "I hear there are new owners at the Palmezzo Vineyard?"

I take a deep breath. On the exhale, I try to let go of my need to save this woman who is not ready to be saved. "It doesn't look like they'll be harvesting this year. Their vines are sick."

Zahara's head cants to the side as she regards the vine. There's a spark of clarity in her intelligent gaze.

"Have you seen vine rot like this before, Zahara? Where there is no internal problem, yet the vine is still sick?"

"No." She shakes her head slowly. "But I have heard tales of it."

"What tales?"

"The land upon which that vineyard sits once belonged to my people."

I knew that bit of history. Arizona has the second-largest percentage of Native Americans in America. Over a quarter of the area of the state is reservation land.

Zahara's mother was a descendant of the Mayan. Her father was a descendant of the Tohono O'odham tribe that once lived and toiled on these lands before the Europeans came. Her grandfather moved their family to Mexico shortly after my grandfather bought this land. They made the trek across the border every year to work the land that once was theirs.

I now realize I'm not sure which branch of her people she is referring to. The indigenous people of

Central America? Or the native inhabitants of North America? Would it be racially insensitive of me to ask? I'm not sure, so I just listen.

"The stories state that my people angered the god of the underworld. The god made it so that nothing would grow atop the soil until his ire was appeased."

"How would the god's ire be appeased?"

"When the Night Son greets the dawn."

I had been taken in by her tale, but now I frown. "Night sun? That makes no sense."

"Of course it doesn't, Ms. Durand. It's just a myth."

14

G*aius*

IF IT WERE MY CHOICE, I'd stay awake all day. I have
no desire to walk into the sun, I just want to be
awake in it. But each night, as the moon goes down
each night, it compels the children of the night to go
down with it. At my age, I can stay up a little later
each sunrise, and wake a little earlier each sunset.

My body begins rousing even before the last of
the sun's rays are creeping down below the horizon.
It's not enough to free me from my daily turmoil.
The nightmare holds fast.

As I sleep, and I try to kick free of the slumber of the dead, I hear her. She is always in the background. The sound of her laughing, of her screaming, of her sighing with pleasure. I would always listen to those sounds to know if it was safe.

The only time I could ever be certain, was when she was writhing beneath me. When Domitia trembled at my hand, I knew a second of safety. When I tamed her with my tongue, there would be a pause from peril, a period of protection. But I always knew the higher she rose on the peak, the sooner she would come crashing down and bring a world of agony down on me.

And so, trapped in the last few moments of my slumber, I rub. I lick. I pump into her with everything I have to keep her on that edge for as long as possible.

Stamina meant a reprieve from the sting. Endurance meant a break from her bite. Virility meant a deferment from discomfort.

Pleasure is not for me. I have to keep my wits, else I lose control of myself and she takes the reins of power. And then there would be real torture.

I know there will be pain eventually. Domitia cannot be happy unless she hurts the ones she cares about. She is a true sadist.

The sounds of her pleasure reach a crescendo. I know that my time is nearly up. The pain is coming.

What will it be this time? Will she pierce my scrotum again, adding a new adornment to my balls? Perhaps a new brand on my flesh? Hopefully this time, she'll use a hot iron and not tear at my skin with her fingernails. Whatever way Domitia decides she'll show her twisted love for me today, I take a deep breath and prepare, knowing there is no escape from her.

She smiles her cruel grin that displays her other-worldly beauty. That grin led a child of the slums to follow behind an older woman and become ensnared in her fangs. She brought me from down low, up to a high place. I never suspected she would thrill in dropping me from on high, over and over again.

Her smile stretches across her face. Her eyes flash. She bares her fangs. I brace for the pain, only to scramble awake.

My mouth is open wide on a soundless scream. My fingers are wrapped around torn sheets. My eyes see the last strands of sunlight setting from the corner of the room.

In the shadows of my bedroom sits a large figure,

huddled in the darkness. My fear does not increase. My anxiety lessens at the sight of him.

"Dreaming of her again?" Virius asks.

I still haven't found my voice, so I do not respond. He doesn't need me to. The three of us have this in common. We all dream of her. Hadrian's dreams are ones of longing and shame. Mine are filled with performance anxiety and pain. Virius? I dare not think of what horrors she put him through. Of the three of us, I know he got it the worst.

Domitia made Hadrian love her. She made me fuck her into senseless pleasure. Virius? Him, she liked to share.

"I still can't believe she is truly gone," says Virius. His chest is bare. He wears only a loincloth wrapped around his hips in the way of his warrior ancestors.

"She is." I find my voice to give my brother the assurance. "I saw her burn this time. There were no tricks."

Lucius had taken Domitia into his dungeons. There, he had exacted revenge for all of them, including the countless young men Domitia had turned over the centuries only to slaughter at whim. Hadrian hadn't been interested in seeing his former love again, now that he had the true love of his life. It had taken days to coax Virius out of the cellars after her return. I had gone to watch Domitia turn to ash for my brothers. She smiled at me one last time as she burned. Her eyes had fluttered as though she liked the pain of death. She probably had.

"Do you think that she will haunt us?" said Virius.

"She could if she had a soul, which she does not. So, we're safe."

Virius appears to turn that word over in his mind. *Safe.* None of us know the definition any longer—if we ever have.

I say nothing of seeing Domitia nightly in my dreams. The only thing that would free me of that apparition would be to stay awake all day. But my skin allergy and need for blood preclude me from accomplishing that feat.

I should get up. But I feel restless. My sleep hasn't been fitful in years.

In times like these, I would reach out for a woman. A submissive female whose pleasure I could control, whose climax I could toy with, whose will I could bend to my fancy. Being in control of a woman's pleasure is the only way I feel safe, both in the sleeping and waking worlds. As long as a pussy is writhing at my command, all is well.

I look over at my brother. Virius is watching me. His dark eyes are clear, the bags heavy under them.

"When's the last time you slept?" I ask.

Virus shrugs his large shoulders. Though we are both compelled by the sun to sleep, that does not mean we ever rest. Viri's eyes are always wide. I can't remember the last time I've seen the man blink. His fists and biceps are always gathered in bulges, as though he's perpetually ready to strike.

"Come." I pat my mattress, scooting over to make room for him.

Virius rises and comes to the bed. The mattress dips as the cushions welcome his big body. He lies down on his back and stares at the ceiling. The tension remains in every cord of his being.

"Rest a while." I place my hand on his shoulder. "I'll watch your back."

Bit by bit, the tension seeps out of his body. The sun has set by the time Virius is softly snoring. I stay awake and watch my brother. It reminds me of the old days when Domitia took in a new pet. During those few weeks, while her attention was diverted, Viri and I stole our rest. We would listen to the moans and screams of her newest toy, knowing that she would soon tire of them and come looking again for her favorites.

Back then, Virius and I would take shifts, sleeping back to back, watching for the dangers of our mistress. Still to this day, I sleep best when I know he is near. Tonight it is my turn to keep watch for as long as he needs.

15

M *arechal*

WHEN I PEER down into the microscope, I worry that the time may have come when I need glasses. The image in the lens is in focus. The specimen is clear to see. And that is the problem.

I pull away to peer down at the Serrano vine without the 400x magnification. The root rot is clear and present on the ends of the vine. But under the lens, I saw... nothing.

That can not be.

I increase the magnification and look again. I get

the same result. There are no wormlike growths attached to the plant's cells. No oblong organisms. The plant looks healthy inside. But on the outside, it is dying.

Is this some kind of joke? If it is, it's an elaborate one. Gaius didn't hand me this vine. I plucked it from the vineyard myself after he… plucked me.

The ringing of my cell phone buries the thought before it can take root in my mind. Looking down at the caller ID is enough to make me drop the plant and jerk away from my tools.

"Cari!"

"Hey, Mare, it's me."

"I know it's you. Where are you?"

"I'm with Hadrian."

Her voice sounds different, raspy, as though she's thirsty. My first thought is what it always is with my younger siblings. "Is he feeding you?"

Cari chokes on the other end of the line. My maternal instincts go into overdrive. I want to hang up and dial 911, but I have no idea where she is, or where the nearest emergency room is. Hadrian better know CPR, or I'll kill him.

My baby sister, whom I've cared for since the day she was born, is gasping for air. But it's not because she's choking. "Are you laughing?"

Cari clears her throat, but another snort escapes her mouth.

"I don't see what's so funny," I say through gritted teeth.

"Just a private joke between me and Hadrian."

"Your kidnapper."

"We're married, Mare."

"You just met him two weeks ago. It's all happened so fast. Tell me, Cari, did he force you to do this?"

"Really?" There's another snort on the other end. "You raised me, Marechal. Do you really think I'd let a man make me do anything?"

Despite myself, I chuckle. We're giggling now, and it feels good. It would feel better if she was standing next to me. I'd reach over and give her a one-armed hug. I'm a couple of inches taller than my sister, so my chin would rest atop her head. I'd turn my face until my nose was in her hair and I'd inhale, catching a whiff of the sweet scent she's carried with her since she was a baby.

"I'm fine, Mare. This is what I want. You've had to take care of me all my life. It wasn't fair to you. Especially this past year when I've been so awful."

"Papa's passing was hard on all of us."

"Yeah," she agrees. "On all of us. And you took

care of me and Arnie. But who's there to take care of you?"

I cross my free arm over my midsection, preparing to tell my baby sister I don't need anyone to take care of me. That I can handle it myself. That I'm just fine.

As soon as the thought flits across my frontal cortex, a familiar weight settles down over my shoulders like a shawl of stones. The heaviness spreads through my body until my feet feel itchy, as though an irritating fungus is growing there. Goose pimples rise on my arms, like the pockmarks on the vine under my scope.

But unlike the vine which looks bad on the outside and healthy on the inside, I am fine. Both inside and out.

"You were with Gaius the other day."

The sound of his name makes the stone shawl slip from my shoulders. The bumps on my arms settle.

"He's a good man," she continues.

My gaze narrows, though I know she can't see me. In the past, Cari has tried to set me up with her middle school gym teacher, her high school AP Chemistry teacher, and her ethics professor from her freshman year of college.

"He could be good for you."

"We're not talking about me, Carignan. We're talking about you."

"I'm so happy, Mare. I want you to be as happy as me."

I don't have time for a relationship. There is always so much on my plate. Since I was a teen, I've been running a business, raising children, and taking care of a household. The few times I dated, those men only served to add to my to-do list—including carving out the time at night to do them.

But last night, Gaius Serrano had taken just a few minutes to do me. Even though I hadn't gotten the muscle clenching written about in a Penthouse fiction story, I had experienced a release. It had been nice. Really nice.

To be taken care of by someone else.

To take off all that weight on my shoulders.

To simply lie back and experience pleasure.

But it had come at a price. One I am not willing to pay again. My integrity is worth more than a few moments of bliss. Isn't it?

"I'll be home soon, Mare. I just need some time to... adjust to my new life with Hadrian. If you need anything, just ask Gaius."

"Cari—"

"Mare, I've gotta go. I'll see you soon. I promise."

The line goes dead. I have half a mind to redial, but I know she won't answer. Cari is right in one regard: I raised her well. No one can make her do something that she doesn't want.

I have to admit that Hadrian didn't kidnap her. I never truly believed it. I just don't like not knowing where she is, or having access to her. That might make me a helicopter sister, but I'll take the title if it keeps my siblings safe.

I straighten my spine as I hang up the phone. The heavy shawl settles back around my shoulders. At least the imaginary weight is enough to hold off the goosebumps on my arms this time.

"There you are."

The sound of his voice loosens the burden wrapped around me. As I turn to face him, the weight falls entirely away. His smoldering gaze is on my heels, making a slow circuitous route up the line of my skirt, over the curve of my breasts, and finally, to my face. Goosebumps have risen on every inch of flesh that Gaius's eyes touched.

He is dressed in an impeccably tailored suit. The fabric shows off his powerful thighs. His long limbs end in expensive, polished shoes. The button is open on his coat. The silk of his shirt clings to his pecs. The muscles under that shirt look enticing, bitable.

Bitable? I give myself a shake. I have never once thought of biting a man. I have never had sexual thoughts about a man. But just the sight of Gaius Serrano standing in my doorway, backlit by the moonlight, makes my libido flare to life like never before.

"See something interesting?" he drawls.

"What? No. Don't flatter yourself, Mr. Serrano. How did you even get in here?"

"You invited me last week."

Last week? When I'd met him and Hadrian for the first time? Why is he referring to that? "I mean tonight. What are you doing here now?"

He motions to the vine under the scope.

"There's nothing there," I say.

"Are you saying there's nothing wrong with my vines?"

"The rot is there. It's clear as the eye can see. But the scopes don't pick up any organisms inside the plant. I've never seen anything like it."

Gaius bends down and peers into the scope. I peer at him as he does so. I'm not sure if it's simply seeing the tight curve of his backside, or if it's watching him handle my tools, but I do see something interesting.

"Hmmm," he says as he straightens.

"Hmmm? There's an unseen pathogen attacking your vineyard and that's all you have to say about it?"

Gaius inhales deeply. His chest rises with the motion. His chest muscles press more firmly against the fabric of his shirt. So much so that I can see the outline of his nipples. My mouth waters, and I ache to run my tongue over them.

I swallow hard, trying to banish that thought from my entire being. This man is my enemy. He holds the fate of my business in his hand. And he's cavalier in his handling of it.

"Perhaps your equipment needs cleaning," he says.

"Excuse me?" Did this man really just call into question the performance of my tools? "There is nothing wrong with my equipment. This is a state of the art lab, and I am meticulous in the upkeep of all my tools."

"I'm sure you are, Ms. Durand. My apologies."

Again, his gaze rakes over me, taking in every detail again even though he already looked me over when he came into the room. I feel like I am now under the microscope of Gaius's lens. I'm certain he can see into the heart of me. That he can tell that I've been fantasizing about him.

"Let me make it up to you. Let me have you for dinner."

He says *have you*, not *take you*. My survival instinct warns me that wasn't a slip of the tongue.

"Is this going to turn into another sex deal?"

"Would you like it to turn into another sex deal?"

Gaius flashes white teeth when he grins. My fight or flight response goes haywire. The survival instinct is telling me to run. But the direction it points towards for safety is into Gaius's arms.

"This is sexual harassment," I say.

"Not if I have your consent."

"You're lording your power over me to get me to do what you want."

"You're right. I am lording my power over you. Because it's what you want."

He steps closer to me. So close, I can smell the salt of the sweat behind his ear. His hot breath has notes of sweet wine. Something dark. Perhaps a Japanese plum wine? A Sémillion grape, maybe?

It makes me think of the blend I've been working on all month: a dessert wine with notes of blackcurrant and raspberries. I'm certain it'll be a hit with the younger college crowd who are just learning to refine their palettes. But will I even be allowed to make it with a purist like Gaius Serrano at the helm of my company?

"The only thing I want from you is my company. But I'm not going to whore myself out to you to get it."

The lazy smile drops from his face. His upper lip crashes into his lower lip like an expensive bottle of wine falling to the floor. "Never use that word in the same sentence as yourself."

"But that's what this is; sexual favors for currency."

"No," he says, his smug smile restored. "The shares are a gift, like a piece of jewelry between lovers."

"We're not lovers."

"No," he says, his smile holding a hint of sadness. "I don't have lovers. Lovers have sex. Intercourse. They fuck."

I don't flinch at his rude words. But between my legs, I am aching and wet. Gaius's nostrils flare as though he can scent that private truth.

"I don't want to fuck you, Marechal. I just want to play with your cunny."

I flinch then. A whoosh of air leaves my mouth just as my nostrils flare to take more in. The result leaves me lightheaded.

"I want to make your pussy throb with want and then weep with pleasure. I want the pleasure from my hands, from my tongue, to rise so high inside of you that you beg me to fuck you."

The silence looms between us. All I can hear is the sound of his even breaths. My own inhales are shallow, but I am able to find my voice. "I'll die before I ask you for anything."

It's the wrong thing to say. I imagine Eve likely said the same thing to the snake before he coaxed her into her own downfall.

"Let's make a deal, Ms. Durand. If I can't make you come ten times tonight, I'll give you back three more shares."

I open my mouth to tell him to go to hell. Only one word comes out. "Six."

Six shares would give me back the controlling interest in my company. I would be back in charge.

"Four," he counters.

"Six," I hold steady.

"Five, and that's my final offer. For tonight."

His voice is like a hiss in my ear. His grin is too

wide. I can see all of his white teeth flashing, like a snake ready to pounce.

I should back away. I should run. If I get in bed with this man, I could lose more than the keys to paradise. I could very well lose my soul.

"Deal."

16

———

G *aius*

Contrary to popular belief, not all vampires fly. But we do all move faster than human perception. Perhaps that's why I like fast cars.

My Venom zips through the city, handling the hairpin turns with ease at eighty miles per hour. Beside me, Marechal is strapped into the passenger seat. I expect her to admonish me for my speed. As the speedometer clicks past eighty-five, she doesn't open her mouth.

Instead, her thighs are pressed together. Her

nails are digging into the leather of the seat. Her chest rises and falls in quick pants. I can see her nipples pebbling beneath her shirt.

Just as I suspected. The tightly wound woman likes being out of her own control and in mine. She might not be a submissive in the sense that she wants a Master to dominate her, but she will hand over her power to me. I just need to show her that I am more than man enough to handle her, just as easily and deftly as I handle this car.

Up ahead, there is a bend in the road. Marechal lets out a slow exhale as I take the curve. Her fingers relax in her lap, as though the worries of the day are slipping loose of her hold. Her back arches as the speed climbs to one hundred. Her sigh harmonizes to the hum of the engine as I zip in and out of the slow-moving domestic cars.

She voices not a single concern. Not a peep of protest. She is the picture of submission as she lets me dominate from my place in the driver's seat.

I would have driven forever. Instead, I drive past the turn that would take us back to the Serrano vineyard and head to town. Marechal's eyes are closed but she is wide awake, fully aware of everything happening to her. From the circulating air in the car, I can smell that she is aroused.

I want to keep her on the edge of this pleasure. I want to make it last for her. And then I will play with her all night until she screams herself hoarse from the pleasure I will bring.

It's been a long time that I was this giddy to play. I have half a mind to turn the car around and head home. The Venom could handle the sharp change in direction. But I want to walk on the edge alongside Marechal.

I ease the car to a stop in a downtown parking lot. This part of town is teeming with youths at this time of night. Marechal opens her eyes and frowns in confusion as she takes in the sight. The fact that she doesn't question me pleases me immensely.

She takes my hand as I open the passenger door. We walk past the line of people waiting to get into the restaurant and are seated immediately in my favorite spot, the best spot in the place. I wave the menus away and order for her. I order a selection of appetizers, an entree, and a dessert. But only enough for one.

As a vampire, I can eat human foods. I can even enjoy them. The only appetite I have this evening is for the woman sitting across from me.

Again, she doesn't argue as I order for her. She sits back and watches my every move, as though she's searching for a weakness and preparing to strike. The only time she sits forward and voices a protest is at my wine selection.

"We'll have the 1990 Château Margaux," I say.

"That only comes by the bottle, sir."

It's a $1200 bottle. I lift my gaze to glare at the server. The waiter takes in my tailored Versace suit and Rolex. He gulps and nods, straightening to go.

"Wait," says Marechal, raising a finger. "I don't care for the Margaux. I'd prefer the 1989 Château Cheval Blanc. And you can put it on my tab."

It's a $1300 bottle. The waiter looks between the two of us. He wisely steps back from the pissing contest going on.

"What's your issue with the Margaux?" I ask.

"The vineyard is on the left bank of Bordeaux. I find the grapes on the right bank, such as the Cheval, are richer."

I can only grin. The woman surprises me at every turn. For someone as old as I am, that is a novelty.

"I thought we were headed to your place?" she says.

"I need to feed you first. You'll need your strength for the work I have planned for you."

Her smile is tight. "Aren't you a gracious boss?"

"I expect you to buy me a mug that proclaims it."

Her snorting laugh is a surprise to us both. It's the most unladylike sound. I wanted to make this buttoned-up, no-nonsense woman do it again.

"Anyway, I wouldn't expect any Employer of the Year awards too soon," she says. "You won't be my boss for much longer."

"That is assuming I don't win our latest bet."

"I don't think you want to win. I think you just want to prove me wrong."

Once again, she tries to peer inside me. I want to tell her that it is a futile exercise. There are no depths to me. I like to eat food. I like to eat pussy. And I like to look good doing it.

"What happens when I get the controlling shares of my company back?"

"Then I won't have anything you want any longer. And you won't have any need to play my little games anymore."

She swallows hard. I can see the knot lodge in her throat. I thrill at the knowledge that she might not want this to end. Which is strange. I never want more from a woman. Hell, I can't remember the last time I sat down for a meal with a woman. Or had a conversation with one.

Marechal fidgets in her chair. I know she's

uncomfortable with the deal we've made. I should've taken her straight to her bed and begun. Hell, I should've laid her out on her lab table and buried my nose in what I know will be a tight cunt. But I love watching her squirm. It'll make her juices all the more sweet; richer than the Cheval wine she now sips at.

"You've never been here?" I ask.

She shakes her head as she toys with her stem.

"You don't flaunt your wealth?"

"Money doesn't interest me. Science does. Advancing my business. Taking care of my family. Handling my responsibilities."

"And shoes."

We both glance down at her crossed legs. They end in designer shoes. Vintage French. I think I might've flogged the designer a few decades ago.

"Are we not going to talk about your sick vines?" she says after the food arrives. "This might be a new disease. One that doesn't penetrate the inner workings of the plant. We need to collect more samples. We could even publish a paper on our findings."

Our findings? Fates, if the woman isn't sexy as sin when she talks science. I hate to disappoint her, but alerting the human population to what's happening in my vineyard is the last thing I'm about to do.

I don't need any human attention on my property. Especially not after what I saw in Marechal's microscope. She couldn't see it with her human vision, but I saw the signs clearly. My family and I might be well and truly fucked. But I'll deal with that later.

"You know, there's a rumor that your land is cursed," she says.

I try not to chew the inside of my lip. It's a habit that shows my annoyance. Instead, I cock my head to the side and regard her. "The scientist believes in curses?"

She doesn't take the bait. But I know her intellectual mind isn't latched onto the idea either. She's just doing what she does best; problem solve.

"When I was a kid, there were stories that if you snuck onto Old Man Palmezzo's vineyard, the vines would eat you up and suck you down into the ground like a Venus Flytrap."

I say nothing to confirm or deny the childhood tales. There are caverns beneath the vineyard in some parts. My brothers and I went down there when we first came here.

"Today, one of my harvest workers told a different story. She said her people used to own the land."

"Her people?"

"She's Native American. Or indigenous? I'm not sure. She said it was her people who angered the god of the underworld, and that he's the one who won't allow anything to grow there until he is appeased by... what did she call it?"

I hold tight to my amused smile, but the prickles are crawling up my back. It must be something really bad to make a vampire's skin crawl.

"Oh, I remember. She said nothing would grow until the night sun greets the dawn. Maybe she means an eclipse?"

"That's some tale."

I keep my features placid. There are all kinds of lores in my world. I don't usually hold truck with curses and myths. But I respect them enough to know that there's often a grain of truth to them. I'll discuss this with my brothers later. Right now, I want to focus on the dessert I've brought to dinner.

"You're not going to eat?" Marechal asks.

"I think I will have an appetizer."

I reach forward and take her left hand. I raise her knuckles to my mouth as though I'm going to kiss them. Instead, I take her index and then middle finger into my mouth.

The fork in Marechal's right hand clanks to her

plate. The restaurant is too full of the hum of dinner conversation for anyone to notice her flub. She doesn't yank her hand from me. She watches with wide eyes and an open mouth.

After I suckle her fingers, I give them back to her. "Put them in your cunt."

She blinks as if she's coming out of a pleasant dream. I can see the moment realization strikes and she comprehends my words. I give her no space to disobey me.

"Now."

17

Marechal

MY FINGERS TREMBLE as they leave Gaius's lips. His tongue is pure velvet, a hot sheath that I now ache to taste. But his mouth closes. His lips press together in a firm line.

"Do it," he commands.

My hand flutters as it glides away from him and back across the table to me. It's my hand. The nails I trimmed and painted a pale coral a few days ago. On my index finger is the scar from an accident with pruning shears when I was a teen.

My hand is capable. My hand is sure. But my hand is no longer my own. It follows this man's command and slips under the table.

The din of the restaurant becomes amplified in my ears. A woman at the table to my right lets out a tittering laugh. To the left, a man is standing, his wine glass lifted to start a toast. The hostess seats a new couple. A waiter's head bobs as he takes down an order. Dishes clatter into a busboy's bin.

Meanwhile, my hand has rucked up my skirt. As my fingers inch up my inner thigh, they leave a trail of Gaius's wetness on my flesh. My mind runs away from me, imagining it's his tongue.

I gasp at the thought.

Gaius grins from across the table.

I'd often wondered why Eve listened to the snake. Later, I learned what a metaphor was. The devil was said to be the most beautiful angel. Easy to see why they changed his character to a spineless creature that slithered on the ground.

"Move your panties aside, *minou*."

There's that pronunciation again. Part of me wants to correct his French. The other part simply wants to listen to his silky baritone make another command.

My fingers do what Gaius tells them to. I shift my bottom on the hard wood of the chair. For a moment, I worry that I sat in a spill. The area beneath me is damp where it wasn't a moment ago. I shudder to realize all that moisture came from me.

"Run your fingers along the seam."

My fingers do as they're told. My index finger starts at the top of my slit. As it moves southward, I feel as though I'm unzipping myself. A cheer goes up to the left of us. The table all raise their glasses as the toast is done.

"Eyes on me."

I jerk my attention back to Gaius. His eyes gleam as they bore into mine. His unwavering gaze makes me feel as though he not only sees exactly what I'm doing under the table, but what it's doing to me inside.

I am coming untethered. Unbound. Unconcerned. Touching myself in such an intimate way in a public space is exciting. But not as exciting as the weightlessness of being under Gaius's command.

"Press your index finger inside that tight, hot sheath, *minou*."

There is resistance when I do so. My sheath hasn't been breached in years. Not by a man, not by me. I have long lost my patience for the fumbling of men down there. I've never had the desire to masturbate. I see now I'll need to rethink both those thoughts.

"Deeper."

I gasp as I comply. My finger presses further. I'm in up to my knuckle.

"Swirl it around, get all the good juices for me."

I do as I'm told. More wetness coats my finger and trickles down into my palm. The sound reminds me of the squishy noise that comes from stomping grapes. My inner walls have the same wet, velvety feel.

"How are you finding everything tonight?"

My back goes rigid as I look over to see the waiter. His gaze is on Gaius and not me. On another night, I would berate the man for his misogynist microaggression. Luckily for him, I have my hands full of other matters.

"Box this up, will you?" says Gaius. "I'm going to finish my meal at home."

The waiter nods and begins removing the plates. Gaius has not taken his gaze off me. I can tell he's waiting to see if I remove my hand. I do not. Even if the waiter wasn't clearing our table, my fingers are sticky with my intimate wetness. And he just took the dinner napkin away.

"Now, give them to me."

My mouth falls open. Of all the things this man has told me to do tonight, this is what shocks me? Slowly, almost reluctantly, I pull my finger from myself. I have to hold myself still on the seat as it's soaked with an even bigger puddle now. I need to get that dinner napkin back to cover the mess I've made, or I can never show my face here again.

When my hand reappears above the table, it glistens in the dim lighting of the restaurant. It feels as though all conversation has stopped and every eye is on my fingers and the shame that coats it. Though what I'm feeling couldn't be called shame. It's too warm, too tingly.

I look to Gaius, waiting for his next command.

He is silent. But the gleam in his eyes shines even brighter. His grins stretches wider. Is that pride?

He leans forward. His lips part. He gazes at me, expectantly. I swallow hard when I realize what he wants me to do.

Once again, my hand trembles as it makes its way to him. I place my index finger on his lip. Gaius's tongue snakes out of his mouth. It captures my finger and sucks it inside. He licks the top, the bottom, and the sides of my finger. The tip of his tongue hardens as it flicks under my fingernail. He hums a low hum of satisfaction that reverberates through my hand. It travels down my body and zings my core, causing little flutters of the muscles.

Was that an orgasm? I'm not sure. A wave of bliss washes over me, and I feel ready to curl into a fetal position and nap.

I can't believe I just did that.

I can't believe I just fingered myself in a dining room and let a man suck the evidence off my fingers. Who the hell am I? And whoever she is, do I want to keep being her?

Gaius's hand is clasped around mine as we leave the restaurant. He's rubbing his thumb over the finger I used to touch myself. He said he would make me orgasm ten times. I don't bother to tell him that he only has nine more times for this night. But I think he knows.

I teeter in my heels on the pavement outside. I've navigated fresh earth in heels. But walking next to this man has turned my legs into a wilting vine.

Am I really doing this? Am I really going to let him fuck me to get the shares back?

If I'm honest, it's not entirely about the shares. I want that pleasure. Not just the pleasure, I want the release. I want that feeling of weightlessness that seems to come whenever he is over me, near me, telling me what to do.

Will he really give me ten orgasms? Is it even physically possible? I know I'm not going to complain while he tries.

He rubs his thumb over the center of my palm. I feel the sensation in my aching core. He could probably finger me with his thumb on my palm and get me off.

This is madness. I've gone insane. And I'm fucking giddy over it.

"Did you just giggle?" Gaius asks.

"I... I think I did."

He looks down at me. My face is upturned to his. I'm a tall woman. One who insists on heels, to boot. His height doesn't make me feel small. It makes him appear capable of handling me.

I'd thought this man frivolous, self-centered, and reckless. He might be all of those things. But when his attention is focused on me, I feel like the center of someone else's world. It's a feeling I'm growing addicted to.

From the corner of my eye, I spy movement. There is something in the shadows. That something has arms and legs, and they're coming at us.

I don't think. I react. I have just enough time to shove Gaius away. But he doesn't budge. Instead, his body blocks mine and I hear a yelp of pain.

I reach for Gaius, already preparing to search for any wound. It's not Gaius who needs my care. Gaius has the body from the shadows pinned against the wall with one hand. In the light of the alley, I see it's a kid. A scrawny kid.

Gaius doesn't appear to care. Those eyes that were gleaming at me a moment ago are filled with rage. His hand is a five-fingered noose around the kid's neck.

"Gaius, it's just a child."

"Men do not attack women," he growls. His voice does not sound human.

"I wasn't going for her," the kid manages to wheeze. "I was going for the bag."

On the ground is the doggie bag of food the waiter had packed for us, along with the two bottles of expensive wine. Only shards remain of the pricey drinks.

"I was grabbing for the food. I wasn't going to hurt anybody. I'm just hungry."

Something flickers in Gaius's eyes. The rage melts away but what it reveals isn't exactly clear. Tendon by tendon, he releases the kid. Before the youth can scurry away with the bruises on his neck, Gaius grabs him by the shirt.

Gaius takes the bag with one hand, still holding onto the kid with the other. He reaches into his pocket and drops a few bills into the bag and then hands it to the youth. The kid's eyes grow wide. The moment Gaius lets him go, he takes off running with his prize.

Gaius stands with his hands in his pocket, watching the kid's retreating form. His gaze is wistful, as though a memory is playing behind his eyes. What memory, I can't imagine. The Serranos come from old money.

"Are you okay?" He turns to me, looking me up and down. His large hands run over my arms and shoulders, checking me much like I would do to them when Cari or Arnie came out of a scrape.

"I'm fine," I say.

His gentle probe turns forceful as he grips my shoulders firmly. "What were you thinking, moving in front of me? Did you think I couldn't protect you?"

My brain is rattled, and it takes me a moment to parse his words from his actions. "I don't know? I wasn't thinking clearly. It was probably my maternal instinct. I've been raising my younger siblings since I was a kid myself. I don't know any other way to react."

Gaius stares at me for a long moment—so long that I begin to squirm under his perusal.

"That was kind of you, to give that kid the food and the money."

He doesn't answer, just rubs a thumb over my lip. "I need to make you come. Now."

18

G *aius*

"Eyes on me."

Marechal's gaze rises from what my fingers are doing to rest on my face. The honey wine color of her eyes makes me feel drunk. I continue unbuttoning her shirt by feel only, unable to look away.

Could she be a witch? Is that why she's making me feel desperate for her? I'm old enough to know that real magic exists in this world. Part of me aches to tell this sexy scientist of the unexplainable things hidden in plain sight so that I might watch her bite her plump lips to parse out an explanation.

I don't bother with any tales of the fantastical. I'm at the end of my rope with the need for her. I'm also at the end of her buttons. I tug her shirttails from her skirt.

Her nipples poke through the lace of her white bra. The buds are dark, like plum wine. I know I'm in trouble if my mouth is watering for such a cheap dessert wine. My dick is throbbing, and now my fangs ache. Marechal doesn't know it, but I'm going to feast on her in more than one way tonight.

I wonder: if she knew of my blood-sucking tendencies, would she insist on putting me under her microscope? Would I become her lab specimen that she would poke and prod? Hell, the thought almost seems appealing if I get to have her attention on me.

Marechal raises her hands to unbutton my shirt. Before she can land on a single button, I catch both her wrists in my grasp. It's an old habit. Though there's an ache in my chest where I want to feel her palms pressed against my flesh, I do not risk it. I cannot. Not if I want to derive any pleasure for myself from tonight. And I do. I plan to get punch drunk off this woman's pleasure.

I reach for the silky belt of one of my robes. Turning her wrists face up, I began to bind Marechal's hands. She looks down at my actions, her dark gaze lighting with need even as she questions me.

"What are you doing?" Her voice is breathy, a quiet hum of excitement.

"What I promised you. Ten orgasms. I have a lot of work to do. I don't want you getting in my way."

With her hands secure, I pull Marechal to me. She tilts her head back as she looks up at me. There is no fear in her eyes, only desire.

It's been a long time since I've been drunk. My supernaturally fast metabolism doesn't allow for it. But looking into her Sémillion grape eyes, I feel intoxicated. It's the only reason I can fathom for what I do next. Because I do something I haven't done in centuries; I take a woman's mouth with my own.

I have tasted the finest wines across the world. Nothing compares to Marechal's lips. She is honey and silk. She is robust and decadent.

Her bound hands are trapped between our chests. Her fingers land softly on my chest. The impact of her small finger pads on my flesh nearly knocks me down.

It's been so long since I've felt a woman's touch. So long since I've craved it. I was still human at the time of my last craving for contact. In the next moment, I came to understand that love was pain, and desire could hurt.

Marechal's nails scraping against my chest should rattle me. Instead, they ground me in the present moment. I hold still, waiting for a vision of Domitia's pale face to intrude. But all I see is golden brown skin. All I feel in the scratch of Marechal's nails is a desire to find purchase.

I need her to know that I won't let her fall. I want her to know that I will only lift her up. So I do. Placing my hands on her hips, my tongue still tangling with hers, I raise Marechal bodily from the ground and toss her back on the bed.

Her long limbs sail through the air. Only to land on the bed with a thud. She is splayed unladylike on the mattress. It had to be done. It was the only way that kiss would end, and I have work to do.

I tug down the zipper of her skirt and shimmy her long legs out of the garment. She is left in her lace bra, soaked panties, and those pointed heels. A decadent dessert that I will gorge myself on.

The bed dips as I place one knee on the mattress. Marechal's breath catches as she watches me prowl up her body. Using her heel, she digs into the mattress and scoots back, away from me. Without her hands, she can't find purchase to move much further, nor much faster. She is bound, at my mercy, and I am on her.

I catch one leg. Holding her heel in the palm of my hands, I slide my fingers up her ankle. She shudders at my touch.

"Be a good girl," I say. "Spread your legs for me."

With a shaky breath, she lets her knees fall open. I could've gotten off right there just from this strong woman following the simplest of commands. I need her begging. I need her panting my name. I need to make her back arch and her pussy quiver until she passes out from pleasure.

Gazing down at her, I take a slow inventory of her body, determining where to strike first. Where to put the pressure to tear her apart, knowing that when she comes back together, she will be stronger. And then I'll do it all again.

I hook my thumbs on either side of her panties. With a tug, the material snaps in two, rendering her bare for my gaze. Her pussy lips are not the rosé I'd imagined. Her intimate flesh is the coppery-red of a Catawba grape, an American variety used not only for wine but also for jams and jellies. The color, on Marechal, makes sense.

She gasps when my fingers find her swollen bud. It took me a second longer than normal because her entire cunt is swollen. I give her light touches because I know she craves a strong hand. I've already proven that I am that hand, that I am more than capable of managing her.

It still galls me that she attempted to protect me from that street vagrant. But it also confuses me. As well as it thrills me. I don't know what to make of it, except that I need to make her shiver with the deep, gratifying pleasure that only I can give her.

Marechal moves in time to my strokes. I keep my finger at the right pressure for my touch to be feather-light. She tries to move her hips closer to me, trying to manage me into what she wants. But I know what she needs.

I use my knees to spread her wider, stopping the rise of her hips. When she begins to whimper, satisfaction pours through me. There is nothing like watching a woman break for me. The trembling starts all too soon.

I keep my touch light and soon, trapped as she is, she is bucking against my hand. The wet sounds of my fingers slipping across her little bud make my mouth water. Her cunt and her mouth are gasping with need. The fat pad of my thumb is drenched as she continues to shake with pleasure. I pet her until she comes down. When she opens her eyes, I confirm the count on the scoreboard for our little game.

"That was number two."

Her eyes widen with realization. Of course, I know she came in the restaurant. I hook her bound hands onto a notch on the headboard. Then I lie down on my belly between her thighs, ready for the game to begin in earnest.

19

M *arechal*

I WISH I knew how to lie. I want to tell Gaius that I didn't come back in the restaurant. That way, I'd have nine more of these delightful little explosions to look forward to.

I am a greedy woman.

But I can barely talk as I watch his head bob up and down between my thighs. I've barely stopped trembling from the last orgasm as his tongue laps up the wetness it brought forth. He licks the creases between my thighs, where the elastic of my panties had dug in. He tugs my labia between his lips, as though my flesh were nothing more than a spoon he's licking a dessert from. The more he licks, the wetter I get. The wetter I get, the more he laps it up. Because that is the sound this tongue makes as he suckles at me. The man between my thighs is a big cat, a panther who is lapping up a treat.

The feel of his lips, his tongue, and even his teeth is too much. I need a reprieve. But I can't close my legs. His big shoulders keep me open for his pleasure. His large hands press me open wider.

He takes long, leisurely licks. His eyes remain open, never closing, as though he can't get enough of what he's seeing.

I have to fight to keep my gaze on him. Each time my eyes flutter, I force them back open, not wanting to miss a single second of this.

When he wraps his lips around the oversensitive flesh at the apex of my sex, I am lost. My eyes shut. My mouth opens. And I scream my pleasure.

I slam my thighs closed as another orgasm explodes. But my thighs meet with Gaius's head. My heels dig into his back. He flexes his shoulders, letting the spikes of my stilettos dig into his flesh.

Slowly, he lifts his head, licking his upper lip as his eyes gleam at me. "Three."

Fuck. I collapse back on the pillow. Greedy as I am, I don't know how I'll take seven more of these. But I want them. I want every single one as my due.

Gaius rises off the bed. Is he stopping? Is he giving up? Maybe I should start cheerleading instead of naysaying because I'm now a believer. With those clever fingers and that wicked tongue, I think he can have me trembling in pleasure for the rest of the night.

But wait? Is that what I want? How exactly did our newest bet go? Do I win if I come ten times? Or do I lose? It doesn't matter. I want more.

I whimper in protest as he comes to standing. I reach out to him, only to remember that my arms are bound. I hadn't even realized he'd done it. I could raise my forearms and lift the knotted tie from the headboard if I wanted. Or I could simply tug until the knot came loose.

I do neither. There's something about the feeling of being bound that makes me feel free.

On the other side of the room, Gaius rummages around in a drawer. I can't see what he has in his hands as he turns. On his way back to me, he stops at an easel and picks up a brush.

When he splays his wares on the mattress, I gasp. My thighs press together, not closing entirely due to the swollen lips he's just kissed. My gaze catches his. The wicked sparkle in his eyes is clear in the low light of the room.

Gaius runs his fingers over a paintbrush; a long dildo that's curved like a U-pipe at the tip; a second toy with a bulbous head that I know is a Magic Wand; and rope.

"What are you going to do with those?" My voice is small, barely above a whisper, and filled with tremors.

"What I promised."

I open my mouth to protest. Nothing comes out. Because I don't have a single objection to his plan. Hell, I don't even question him about his strategy— because I want whatever he's going to do to me.

Gaius reaches for my hands and unties the belt. Disappointment rushes down my arms along with the blood as I regain my mobility. Now that I'm no longer restrained, questions about his intentions flood my brain.

Is he going to put those dildos inside of me? What's the purpose of the one that's curved? The Magic Wand definitely won't fit inside me, and I'd prefer his tongue again. And what's with the paintbrush?

I don't ask a single question because when I look

up, he's smiling at me. As though he's anticipating every one of my queries.

"You are a very naughty girl, aren't you, Marechal?"

I shake my head, no. I'm a good girl. I always do what is expected of me. I do not shirk from my responsibilities. I can feel them coming back down on my shoulders now that I'm free of the belt.

"You like being bound."

It's not a question, so I don't answer. I'm sure he knows how I feel. At every turn, he seems to know exactly what I need.

Gaius takes the rope in one hand and one of my thighs in the other. He begins to loop the rope around my knee.

"What are you doing?"

"Shhh," he soothes. "I'm going to take care of everything. You just lie back and relax."

He finishes the knot above my knee and then reaches for my arm. He makes the same loops just above my elbow and then affixes a knot between my two limbs. He goes to the other side of the bed and does the same with my left arm and knee. When he is finished I am laid open, like a spider on her back with her limbs splayed. Once more, I feel light and free.

Gaius smiles down at his handiwork. Then he leans down and kisses me. A light brush of his lips against mine. I taste myself on his lips. I swallow down the kiss and then arch for more.

He gives me what I want: slowly, languidly kissing me with my legs open, my pussy throbbing, and my nipples tight, achy points. He doesn't touch me anywhere, except his lips against mine, his tongue lapping at mine.

If this goes on, I think I'll come from it. But he breaks the kiss. I gulp down air.

"You were close, weren't you?"

I open my eyes. He's gazing down at me with wonder. I want to be a wonder to him.

"I could watch you come all night, *minou*. I'm going to."

He picks up the brush. Is he going to go back to the easel and paint me? I think I would die of want if he did.

He doesn't move from the bed. Instead of dipping the brush in any paint, he places it on his tongue and licks the bristles. My pussy jumps knowing exactly what that felt like.

Gaius's attention turns from my face to my bared pussy. He tilts his head, regarding my aching labia like I am a work of art he's trying to interpret. Placing the soften bristles against my core, he begins to paint.

"Such a pretty *minou.*"

That's when I get it. He was never calling me a cat or a kitten. He was calling me another word entirely.

The brush strokes feel nothing like his tongue. His tongue was at times a soft velvet touch, and at others, a stiff tip. The paintbrush has many bristles; soft at the edges and firm at the center. They all touch me at the same time. The bristles are concentrated at my clitoris. The small bud of nerves is having trouble processing all the sensations. It's going to spontaneously combust any second now.

"Try to hold it for me, *minou.*"

"I can't," I pant. "I want it."

"I'm going to give it to you. Again, and then again. But hold back for now."

His words make no sense. I don't try to comprehend. There are too many sensations happening to my body. I can't close my legs to relieve some. I can't grab hold of anything to hold onto. I can only feel, and I am overwhelmed.

"Trust me. I know how to take care of you."

There are those words again. I hold my breath, trying to clamp down on the tingles that are rolling through me. They're picking up speed and heat and intensity. Pretty soon, those tingles are a blazing, fiery freight train about to burst out of me.

"You're so beautiful when you're close. Hold out, *minou*."

But I can't. My grip is loosening. One finger lets go. Then another. And then I am crashing, falling, undone.

20

G *aius*

I RUN my hands over Marechal's nipples. The tiny jewels scrape against the flesh of my palms. The buds are puckered so hard, they could cut glass.

Her eyes are closed, her head lolling. She is in total bliss, and has been since the sixth orgasm. That was three orgasms ago. One to go.

"Marechal, open your eyes."

Her lids flutter. But they do not open. She is conscious, aware. I have worn her out. However, I know she has more in her.

"Look at me."

Her lids lift, revealing those plum eyes that leave me feeling tipsy every time she glances my way. "Gaius," she sighs, before closing her eyes again.

My chest rises at the reverence she puts in my name. I feel like a king, a conqueror. I've broken many women to my will. Marechal is my greatest prize.

Though I made it bend, there's still steel in her spine. A small smile touches her lips. In it is a smirk of defiance. It tells me that though I may have conquered her body, there's still a reserve inside that I will never touch.

My fingers twitch. My palms itch.

I look again at my handiwork. Her body is perfection in the candlelight. The flame plays off the honey of her skin.

My cock throbs in my pants. But I don't want in her mouth. I want inside of her. I want passage into her core, to tap that reserve.

I haven't fucked a woman's cunt in… I can't remember the last time. For so long, women have only been for food and fun. But this one? This one, I want to see me. This one, I want to speak to me. This one, I want to touch me.

I undo the knots at her knees. My hand trembles

as I do so. Once she's free, she could strike out. She could inflict pain upon me. That's what happens after a woman is sated.

For the last hundred years, I've never bothered to test the theory. I have another tend to the aftercare of my playthings. I'm gone before they come out of subspace. But there is no one else here but the two of us. Because I've never taken a woman to my bed... ever.

I didn't want to bring Marechal to the club. For so many reasons. I didn't want any of the others to see my fascination with her. I didn't want them to think she was fair game after I am done with her.

Done with her?

I am not done with her. My throbbing dick tells me so. Still, I untie her.

To let her go?

To see if she'll stay?

To prove she'll strike out?

As I set her hands free, they go limp at her sides. She is far too blissed out to lift even a finger. I look down at this strong woman, who stood toe to toe with me in business matters and didn't flinch. At this moment, I have all the power. I can do anything to her that I want. She has no power to stop me. She couldn't even form the words to say no. She is powerless. So how does she still hold so much power over me?

I work the kinks out of her legs and arms. I've been edging and tormenting her for hours. Her cunt is a darker shade of red from my abuse with the G-spot dildo and Magic Wand vibrator. As I'd plunged the bulbous head into her over and over again, I'd imagined it was my cock thrusting into her. The thought had made my fangs ache.

They ache now, reminding me I haven't eaten today. I haven't eaten since yesterday, when I first had a taste of Marechal. I know her blood will taste as sweet as her cunt.

"Did I win?"

My gaze shoots to her. Her eyes are still closed. There is a smug grin on her lips.

"Thought you'd tapped out," I say.

"I'm still in it. There's no way I can have another orgasm. My body is numb."

"Challenge accepted."

She chuckles, eyes still closed. She lifts a limp hand. My breath stops at the sight of it. I hold still, motionless as it aims for me.

What will she do? Will she strike me across the face? Will she dig her claws into my nipples? Will she punch my balls?

Marechal's hand lands on my cheek. The soft impact nearly knocks me over. Instead of pulling away as instinct dictates, I lean into her.

"Gaius," she sighs. "Kiss me."

I do. I press my lips to hers. Her body stirs beneath me. Something in the back of my mind wriggles, warning me that this is dangerous. That I will pay for this caress. That pain will follow.

Pleasure blooms inside me as her other hand presses against my chest. I smell her blood racing through her limbs, heating up as I take her lips with mine.

My cock presses against the swollen lips of her cunt. My every instinct tells me to push inside her. But then I would be lost.

I continue to kiss her. I rub my cock against her. I plunge my tongue into her the way I want to work my cock inside her.

Marechal moans into my mouth. She makes no intelligible sound, but I swear I hear her claim me. My hips thrust faster against her; I'm coating myself with her juices.

She breaks the kiss and pulls back. Fear pulls me from her. Is it coming now? The strike for taking these liberties?

"Gaius," she whimpers, throwing her head back as she comes.

I throw my head back as well. I buck against her, letting my seed run between her folds. My balls are empty. I do not have enough blood in me. For the first time in my long life, I feel satiated.

"You win," she says before curling into me and falling asleep.

I hold her to me. No restraints between us. At this moment, I know that I will protect this woman with everything in me.

21

―――――

M *arechal*

I FEEL the first rays of the morning touch my cheek. The sun's light isn't soft, it's harsh. When I open my eyes, I see that it is not the morning sunlight that has awakened me. It's late afternoon.

I have slept most of the day away. Nearly all of my workday. But I feel no sense of urgency to rush from Gaius's bed.

I feel tethered to the mattress even though my hands are no longer bound. The memory of his dominance, of his possession, holds me in my place.

His absence is what finally gets me to shift into total awareness.

I sit up in the bed. There's not a stitch on me except the soft silk of his sheets. The rich oak smell of his surrounds me.

The frame of his bed is made of wood. It's the wood of a Quercus robur, a French oak used to barrel Bordeaux wines. The rich scent has been on my tongue all night. My fingers trace the rings of the carved wood. This tree was old. I can tell by the number of growth rings.

Pinned to the wood is a note. I open it to reveal Gaius's slanted script. My eyes slide over the words, not taking in any meaning the first time I read. I'm too enamored with his handwriting. These days, I don't see much writing in cursive. This is not the cursive I learned in grade school. Gaius's writing calls to the old world, and it's written in French.

Ma petite minou, it begins. I blush now that I know what that word means. The man is brazen to use it as an endearment. But my *minou* warms at the mention.

In the note, he tells me that he didn't want to wake me. He stayed with me as long as he could, but he has obligations for the day. He tells me I'm beautiful. And then the bastard tells me that I snore prettily.

Delight and agitation war within me. I shouldn't feel any of this. The truth is, I don't know what I should be feeling. I experienced more pleasure last night than most women feel in a lifetime. I am no longer in that seventy-five percent of women who don't orgasm. I'm pretty sure I'm now in the top one percentile who can have multiple orgasms. Definitely one of few who have gotten off with a paintbrush.

At the end of the note, he tells me that a driver is waiting outside to take me home. And then he requests the pleasure of my attendance at sundown, like he is some French courtier who is wooing me. The man confounds me. At times, his manners seem so out of place with the present, like he was cut from an ancient cloth. And then in the next moment, he tosses me down and buries his head, or his fingers, or some device, between my thighs and whispers the filthiest things in my ear.

Gaius Serrano does not woo; he takes. He should be done playing with me. What more do I have to offer him?

I dress, pulling on my skirt and shirt from the

other day. They are hanging neatly on a closet door. I can't help myself. I peer inside.

It's clear the man likes decadence judging by the expensive fashion in his closet. Everything is name brand with signs of tailoring. There are exquisite paintings on the walls.

Three men dressed in Roman togas standing on a vineyard. The males bear a striking resemblance to the three Serrano brothers. Next to the Roman rendition is a portrait of the same three men, this time in Renaissance flare. They, too, stand in a vineyard. A final painting clearly depicts Gaius and his brothers in suits. But something is off about the suits. They look vintage.

At the bottom of the third painting, I make out a signature. It is in the same script as the note Gaius left me. Did he paint these pictures? The man has some talent. No wonder that paintbrush seduced me.

The silence in the house is eerie. Though it's fully furnished with extravagant decor, it feels like a crypt. A chilly breeze follows me down the halls, like when I'm walking in a graveyard. There's no life moving, but my spirit doesn't feel alone.

Outside the front door is a sleek town car. The

driver inside is napping. He rouses to attention when I pull open the back door. I curl into the backseat as he pulls away from the Serrano vineyard, feeling sedate and full of energy at the same time.

Halfway home, I nearly tell the driver to turn around. The closer I get to my property, the less sedate I feel. With each passing mile, a to-do list grows in my head. I turn on my phone to open a checklist app when an alert pops on my screen.

It's an email from my accountant. He's attached a ledger that shows one hundred shares of Durand Vineyard are now in my possession.

I refresh the screen, certain I'm reading that wrong.

But no. There it is. Fifty-five shares were transferred into my name early this morning. Not the five Gaius had acceded to.

So that's it? We are done? There is no more need to play this game, so why does he want to see me tonight? For the pleasure of my attendance?

The car pulls to a stop outside my home. I climb out of the back before the driver can come around to open the door. Instead of going inside, I trudge around to the vineyard.

It's late in the day. The harvesters are already here, catching a bit of daylight as they begin to pluck the grapes from the vines. They're in the furthest pasture. Looking around, I see that most of the vines are bare of fruit. It normally takes a couple of weeks at least to clear these pastures. At this rate, they'll be done in a couple of days.

I take sure steps on the fertile soil, the stems of my vintage heels never once sticking in the earth. It's as though the vineyard knows I'm back in command.

I pause as I come up to the group of women bent over baskets. They're all dressed in colorful blouses and skirts. Each of their hair is a plaited braid of ebony. All of their skin is a dark honey gold, a few shades richer than mine.

The woman closest to me lifts her head and meets my gaze. She is older. I can only tell that by the crow's feet at the edges of her eyes. She has no gray, and no wrinkles otherwise. She simply looks as though she's seen far more years than her fit body lets on.

She opens her mouth to speak, but a male voice cuts her off.

"Yes, Ms. Durand? What can I do for you?"

I turn to see one of the few males who have come with the group this harvest. The men, too, all share the same ebony hair with plaits. Though they don't dress in such colorful clothing. Unlike the women, the males all wear dark pants and dark t-shirts. They look more like a security detail than migrant workers. I'm fairly certain this is the same man who spoke so tersely to me just a few days ago.

"Where's Zahara?" I ask, wanting to take the man down a notch, but also, not wanting to give him the time of day. I shouldn't fire him just because I think he's a chauvinist pig.

I could, though. Because I'm the boss.

"Zahara is indisposed today."

I don't like the tone of his voice. He makes the word *indisposed* sound like she's been a naughty girl and is in time out.

"I have a business matter to discuss with her," I say.

"You can deal with me."

"I prefer to speak with management," I say, looking him up and down. "Not the middle man."

The sun is setting but I feel a wave of heat brush my shoulders. A low growl sounds from somewhere close. There are mountain lions in these parts. A few jaguars have been known to walk the land as well. But too many humans dot the fields for them to make an appearance.

When I give the man before me back my attention, his eyes are narrowed slits. His mouth is pinched in disgust. His nose is wrinkled as though he smells something foul on my person.

He opens his mouth to speak, his lips set in a snarl. But a feminine voice cuts him off.

"Zahara isn't feeling well today, Ms. Durand," says the older woman—Itzel, I believe her name is. She's still on the ground, her head down, her gaze averted. "She is resting."

I don't believe Itzel. But it's clear she's trying to break the tension between me and the male. I also get the sense that she's trying to protect Zahara. If I find out it's from this man, I will not hesitate to call the authorities. I know Zahara has all the correct paperwork to be here. I don't know about this man, and I couldn't care less if he ends up in an ICE detention facility with his attitude.

"When Zahara is feeling better, would you tell her that I'd like to see her?"

It's a furtive move, but I see her glance out the corner of her eye at the male. "Of course, Ms. Durand."

I plaster on a friendly, non-combative smile. It makes my teeth hurt. "Thank you both. Thank you all for the hard work you've done this season. I couldn't have done it without you."

The man's shoulders relax a fraction in response

to my dulcet tones. He nods and then turns on his heel, but he doesn't go far.

I bend down to examine a vine. My gaze fixed on the plant, I pitch my voice. "If she's in trouble, you can tell me. I'll help."

A small smile plays at Itzel's mouth. It reminds me so much of Zahara's hard-won grins. I wonder if this is her aunt?

"It's nothing like that," she says. Her gaze turns discerning, as though she's trying to determine if she can reveal a secret. "Zahara is expecting."

Oh? That's not what I was expecting to hear. My gaze slides over to the man. He has his back to us, but I get the eerie feeling that he can hear us even though we are whispering.

"Does she need anything?" I try to push every possible meaning into that one word.

"No." Itzel smiles sadly. "She is simply doing what she was born to do."

I don't believe that. I don't believe that women were solely born to bear children. But I've stepped on enough cultural norms today.

I make my way back to the house. I don't have much time before the sun sets and my own gentleman will come calling. There's mounds of paperwork to do and plans to make now that the business is back under my full control.

Instead of going to my office, I decide to take the rest of the day off. The notion of taking a rare day to myself isn't what surprises me. The fact that I don't feel an ounce of guilt does.

22

G*aius*

"I'D RATHER A WITCH OVER A SHAMAN," I say.

"I'd rather neither," says Hadrian.

I've told my brothers of the magical interference happening in our vine roots. We knew the previous owner had had problems with his crops, but we'd assumed it was due to his own ignorance. Together, my brothers and I have hundreds of years of knowledge and experience making all terrains of soil yield to our will. But this is our first curse.

"If we do nothing, the entire crop will die. We'll lose millions."

"We have billions." Hadrian shrugs. "Besides, I'd rather go home. This Arizona dry heat makes me itch."

"Do you think Cari will want to leave her sister?"

Hadrian grinds his molars. He's too busy teeth-gnashing to see that my hand balls into a fist at the thought of leaving Cari's sister. The sun set over an hour ago, and I'm itching to get to Marechal. But family first.

"The Alpha wolf in these territories is mated to a seer," I say. "I'll reach out through Frangelico, see if she can help us."

"Fine." Hadrian pushes off his chair. "If that's all—"

"That is not all." I raise my hand to stay him. "There is still the matter of the upcoming festivities at Club Toxic."

Hadrian slumps back in his chair with a huff. I look to Virius on the other side of the room.

"I won't go," Viri huffs. He sits on a wine barrel and crosses his arms over his chest. "You know I hate parties."

I try to rein in my annoyance at my brother. Viri would look like a petulant child if he weren't dressed in jeans and cowboy chaps, and a t-shirt that depicts Crazy Horse, a Native American legend. As usual, the top half of his attire is at odds with the bottom half. Sending him as an emissary to greet a congregation of vampire royalty is not the best idea, but it's the only one I have.

"Someone needs to greet the envoy," I say.

"Send Hadrian," says Viri.

"He has to watch Cari."

"I can watch Cari," said Viri.

From the corner of the room, Hadrian growls at that. Newly mated vampires do not take well to other males being alone with their women. Not even their brothers.

"What?" says Viri. "You think I'll fuck her? I lost my taste for cunt after the last Inquisition. I haven't had a cockstand in two centuries. I think it might be broken."

Viri tugs at the waistband of his jeans and peers inside.

"Do not take that out," I warn.

"He needs to look at it and see for himself," Viri says in his most helpful tone.

Hadrian hops up from the chair and backs away. Viri follows his brother around the room, holding his junk for inspection.

"I'm not looking at your prick," Hadrian shouts.

"It's not even hard enough to prick something," Viri insists. "Look. See for yourself. I'm no threat to Cari."

"Put it away, Virius."

I pinch the bridge of my nose. This is my life. For the last couple of centuries, I'd been the only one interested in cunt. Both Hadrian and Virius were too broken to even look at women. Now, I have no interest in any cunt but one.

I let my mind drift back to just before dawn. I'd stayed up as long as possible, watching Marechal sleep. Hers was the slumber of a very satisfied woman.

I couldn't sleep at all. I could hardly blink. I didn't want to miss a second of her lying in my bed.

With her comatose, I took her hand and pressed it to my face. Her fingertips weren't all softness. There were a few ridges from hard work.

As she dozed, I ran her fingertips over my forehead. Pressed them against my eyelids. Held them to my lips. I could not get enough of her touch, and while she slept, I allowed myself to overdose on the sensations.

How had I lived centuries without this feeling? Letting my cheek rest in the palm of her hand, I felt certain I could fall asleep just like that. I didn't. I didn't want to miss a second of the feeling.

So I simply lay there with her. Holding her hand to me. Gazing down upon her softened features. Listening to the soft snore that tickled her nostrils.

Once day began to break, I held out for as long as possible. But the sun's pull was powerful. I rose from the bed and crawled under it. Slipping into my crypt beneath the bed, I could still smell her. With the scent of her in my nostrils, I slipped into my first dreamless sleep in years.

"If Cari touched my cock, it would glide against her hand. Not prick her."

Hadrian, who had been tracing away from Viri, halts. He becomes fully corporeal as he does an about-face. "You want to rub your tiny dick on my woman?"

"My dick isn't tiny. You'd know, if you took a moment to look at it."

Hadrian roars, preparing to pounce on his brother. I trace between the two, placing a firm hand on Hadrian's chest to keep him from murdering Virius. I take care not to touch Viri anywhere at the moment. Hadrian's fangs are dripping. Virius is too busy eyeing his junk to notice.

"New idea," I say. "Hadrian, why don't you take Cari, and the two of you go to greet the envoy?"

Hadrian takes a deep breath, putting his fangs away. Virius looks up, finally putting his junk back in his jeans.

"I don't know," says Hadrian. "She's still so young."

"She'll be around other shifters and vampires," I say. "She can't hurt them. Much."

We have only been in the country for less than a year, but every supernatural creature has heard of Lucius Frangelico's *All Soul's* events. The parties at his club are legendary, calling vampire royalty from all over the world to come to see for themselves.

Since Frangelico is heading out of town on a honeymoon with his new bride, he asked that we help his lieutenants greet some of that royalty. Any other time, I would be delighted to play politics with the high-fanged. But my attention is diverted.

Partly to the issue of our rotting vines.

Mostly to when I can get my hands back on Marechal Durand. And have her hands on me.

"All this so you can stay and check on the vines?" says Hadrian.

"He's not checking on the vines. He's going to wet his wick with Marechal." Virius goes to the fridge behind the bar and rummages through the blood bags in there. "Didn't you hear them last night?"

Now I want to chase the man around the room, but I doubt Hadrian will hold me back. Because Hadrian will likely be chasing after me.

"I told you not to toy with Marechal," says Hadrian. "She's your sister."

I hold up my hand, palm facing out, to halt that nonsense. "Marechal is not my sister. She's…"

The two males wait for me to finish. Hadrian crosses his arms over his chest like he's preparing to protect his bride's sister. Viri holds the blood bag to his lips, as though preparing for a toast.

I lose the train of my sentence. I'm not sure where I was just headed. I don't have the word for what Marechal is to me.

"If you hurt Cari's sister, you will be hearing about it from her for centuries," says Hadrian. "This is why I told you not to toy with Marechal."

"I'm not toying with her," I insist.

"He's not," Viri agrees. "She slept here last night. In his bed. With him beside her. And she wasn't tied down."

I turn on Viri. "You spied on us."

Viri shrugs. "I had a nightmare."

My compassion for my brother wars with my ire

at him coming into my room when I was with Marechal. Though I'm not sure when he did. I was awake nearly all night.

"You didn't hear me when I came in," Viri says after a swig of the blood bag. "You were asleep. I've never seen you sleep that deeply. I've never seen you sleep with someone. Other than the times Domitia crucified you to the bed, of course."

A shudder goes through the room at the mention of her name. Hadrian rubs the black ring on his left finger. Cari had insisted on wedding rings. Viri downs the rest of the blood. I scratch at my palms, remembering what the stakes felt like when Domitia had pinned me down.

"That's the second time Marechal was here," says Hadrian. "You never do repeats."

I don't. There are far too many women to sample. And here I am, anxious to return to this one tonight. So much so that I'm willing to neglect my duties.

"What's going on with you?" Hadrian looks me in the eye. From the rise of his brow, I know I'm not hiding my feelings.

"I just want her again. I didn't get enough the last time."

"Of her blood?"

"I didn't drink from her. I just... want to be with her."

To feel her underneath me. To feel her hands on me. To be inside her.

My two brothers eye me. Not with suspicion. Not with pity. With awe.

"What?" I say.

"Do you think... could this be..." But Hadrian trails off.

"What?" I demand.

"He thinks you're falling in love with her," says Viri.

The sound of something crashing outside the door turns all our heads around.

"That would be Cari," says Hadrian. "She's probably calling Marechal right now. You won't catch her. Best to go face Marechal with this."

But is that what I'm feeling? Love? I've never felt the like before. Not for anyone but my brothers.

For them, I would run into certain danger. I would give my last drop of blood. I would face the sun.

Would I do the same for Marechal?

23

M *arechal*

As I swirl the liquid in my glass, the dark red of the wine catches the light. The taste on my tongue is bold, lusty, full-bodied, yet somehow clean and pure. There's a depth to the Serrano vintage that can only be brought forth by time and age.

With my right hand, I lift the glass to my mouth for another sip. With my left, I lift the vine to glance at the plant. It's been out of the dirt for days now, and it shows no sign of dying.

There are techniques to pluck the vines from the

ground, then air-dry them for months, causing the plants to shrivel—much like hanging dried flowers for decorative purposes. When done with a grapevine, the technique causes the grape to lose its water mass, which increases the alcohol content of the resulting wine.

The Serrano vine, whose grapes haven't even flowered, isn't shriveling. It hasn't lost any water mass since I plucked it the other night. The pimple-like splotches are increasing. In fact, they look like they're growing, like the disease is spreading, along with the plant that isn't receiving any sunlight or nutrients from the earth.

It should not be possible. But the facts are in the palm of my hand. No science supports what I am witnessing. Could this be the curse Zahara spoke of? It wouldn't matter if it is. I don't believe in magic.

I take another sip of the red wine. It hits my tongue chilled but quickly warms, spreading a buzzing heat through my mouth that slides down my tongue. Images of Gaius sipping from my lips, delving his tongue inside me—everywhere—light my mind.

The memory of his fingers on my flesh brings goosebumps to my arms. Tingles ripple across my legs. Embers spark between my thighs.

I remind myself that I do not believe in magic. But the simple thought of that man calls me a liar.

I raise the glass to my mouth again, eager for more of the sensation. The glass is fully empty. I could pour another from the bottle, which is half full.

Gaius's note said he'd be here at sunset. That was over an hour ago. I was never the type of woman to wait on a man. I was always too busy to be bothered.

However, today, I took the day off. I walked past the stack of paperwork on my desk. I turned off the office phone's ringer and let all calls go to voicemail. I kicked off my shoes, pulled up a lounge chair on the back porch, and simply sat all day. Looking out at the vineyard, my vineyard, as the clouds moved across the sky and the sun sank was the most peaceful day of my existence.

I am back in control. I am back in charge of my life. There is no one to tell me what to do or—

My cellphone's ring is shrill in the quiet of the night. I drop the wineglass as I dive for it. The glass cracks but it doesn't shatter.

"Mare?"

"Oh. *Coucou*, Carignan." This past year, the sound of my sister's voice over the phone only brought worry. This is the first time it's brought disappointment.

"Hey there, yourself."

"How are you, *mon chou*? Where are you?"

"I'm at home."

That gets my attention. I sit up in the chair, whirling around as though I can see her coming into the house. "You're here?"

"No—no," she stutters. "I mean, I'm back in the room. At my hotel. With Hadrian. We spent the day out."

I can tell my sister is lying to me. Cari has never been one for minute details unless she's telling a story. Why is she lying now when she says she says she's so happy in her new life? Likely the same reason I started drinking after the sun went down and there was no ring at my doorbell of a French gentleman coming to request my attendance.

"Mare, listen." Cari's voice takes on the rushed, squealing quality from when she was back in high school, on the phone gossiping with her little girl-friends. "I overheard Hadrian talking to Gaius."

"What did I tell you about eavesdropping?" It's so easy to slip back into maternal mode, even though I'm dying to know what Gaius said. "Wait, is Gaius with you two?" Is that why he didn't show at sundown?

"No. They were talking on the phone. Hadrian was on his cell phone. He had it on speaker. While I was in another room—the bathroom. So I overheard."

Lots of detail. Another lie.

"They were talking about you, Mare."

Cari lets the silence linger. I bite my lip, warring between finding the lie and learning the details.

"But you're right," Cari singsongs. "You did raise me not to gossip. So..."

"Spill it, you little brat."

Cari giggles. I realize how much I've missed that sound. For the past year, since our father died, I haven't seen my sister smile. I definitely haven't heard her laugh. She's hiding something, but her happiness is real. I'll get the truth out of her later. Right now I need her to spill the T.

"He really likes you, Mare. Like, *likes you* likes you."

I try to swallow. "What exactly did you hear?"

"I know you slept in his bed last night."

My forehead connects with my palm as I groan. So, Gaius is a kisser as well as a teller.

"No, no, Mare. You don't understand. Gaius is a player—"

"That, I understand."

"He doesn't sleep with women. He screws them. Usually at the club—"

"What club?"

"—but he never brings them home. Or sleeps with them, like lying down in the same bed. He did that with you."

I'm not sure what to think about all this. The man I'm interested in is a confirmed player, who apparently screws women in a club, and has never committed. On the flip side, I'm practically a prude, who rarely leaves her vineyard and has never cared enough to engage in a relationship. Don't we sound perfect for each other.

"Gaius told Hadrian he couldn't get enough of you. Hadrian thinks he might be falling in love with you."

I forget how to breathe. I swallow, and the sweet tang of the Serrano red wine left on my tongue goes straight to my head.

"It's possible, Mare. It happened fast with me and Hadrian. He said he knew the first time he saw me that I would be his."

My mind latches onto those words. The possessiveness of them. Thinking of the words coming from Hadrian's mouth in reference to my sister draw my ire. But when Hadrian's face and voice are replaced with Gaius referencing me, my heart is in my throat.

"The two of you are so alike. Gaius has held his brothers together through some truly awful things in their lives. You've done the same for me and Arneis. I think you two deserve each other. You need to let someone else take care of you for a change."

A sense of peace rushes over me at the thought of Gaius taking charge of me. My head feels light, which is apt, as all the worries have skirted away. My shoulders settle back into the chair; not an ounce of heaviness touches them. When I look up out into the moonlit sky, I see a dark form walking towards me.

My every instinct is to run to the man. To fall down on my knees when I get to him. To spread my thighs and offer him passage into the deepest, most secret part of me.

"I've gotta go, Cari. He's here."

24

G*aius*

I WALKED ALL the way here. But walking is a relative term for someone like me. My feet moved fast across the varied lands. Crunching swiftly over dry patches of desert, then squishing into fertile pastures. Neither the cracked earth nor the lush terrain slowed me down in my efforts to get to Marechal.

Cari had just picked up the phone when I'd left the house. She and her sister's conversation couldn't have taken more than five minutes, even though we live a twenty-minute drive distance from each other.

I hear Marechal's voice before I see her. When she comes into my line of sight, she steals my breath.

Marechal sits barefoot in a lounge chair. Instead of her usual fitted skirt and buttoned-up shirt, she's wearing a white sundress. Her dark hair is loose around her shoulders. Her face is devoid of any makeup. She looks like a virginal sacrifice. I am the monster who will most certainly lay her out on an altar and feast on her this night.

My feet move steadily towards my prize, the treasure that I covet. I'm barely aware of the plants, animals, or other beings around me. Barely aware, but not entirely oblivious.

It's the stillness of the night that catches my attention. The vineyard should be teeming with the sounds of nightcrawlers. Squirrels, raccoons, rabbits, possum, maybe even a few deer should be poking around in this lush buffet now that the sun has gone down. I scent not a hair or bushy tail. Yet eyes flash at me in the dark.

Eyes at eye level. Not from the ground or under bushes.

A couple dozen women stare at me from the rows of vines. They all have baskets in their arms and ripe grapes in their hands. Cari mentioned that the Durands had moved to night harvesting a few years ago. What she didn't mention—because as a human she will not have known—was the fact that her workers are shifters.

Vampires and shifters have a contentious relationship at the best of times, blood-soaked at the worst. The majority of shifter species aren't at the top of the predatory chain. There are plenty of foxes, minxes, and high-tailed bunnies who play at Club Toxic. But there are wolves, bears, and lions that make their home in these parts as well.

Lucius struck a deal with the alpha of this territory not long ago. I get another whiff of these women and I note they do not smell like wolves. I can't place their breed, and I don't intend to ask.

Not a single one takes a defensive stance as I approach. They make no signs of aggression. But neither do I smell an ounce of fear on them.

From the darkness of their hair, the rich tan of their complexions, and the patterns on their colorful clothing, I assume they are Native American. I don't know much about the tribes here, having been born in sixteenth-century Europe. I wonder if they know anything about the magics in my soil? They likely do. Due to their tight-lipped and watchful expressions, I doubt they'll clue me in.

That's a matter for another night. Tonight, my

business is with the mistress of this land. From what I can see of the cleared vines, these workers are loyal to Marechal. Or perhaps to her money. I don't sense they mean her any harm. They're likely just here for the paycheck. We supernatural beings still need to work for our living.

Right now, I just want to live in this moment with the angel on the porch.

"I think you two deserve each other." Cari's voice is clear to me over the phone line, as if she's standing next to my ear. "You need to let someone else take care of you for a change."

"I've gotta go, Cari. He's here."

I have seen women naked. I have seen them in artfully placed strips of fabric that draw the eye. I have seen them bound by rope. I have seen them dripping with my cum all over their faces and breasts. The sight of Marechal, flushed, and mostly covered, has my dick instantly hard.

"Hello," she says. "You said sundown. I wasn't sure you were—"

I stop her talking with my mouth. I'm leaning down over her, crowding her in the chair. She lets her head tilt back, offering me her surrender as I wrap my arms around her. I lift her to me as I plunge my tongue into her mouth. Her ass is not a perfect fit in my palms. Some of her flesh spills over my fingers. I need to sink my fangs into that excess soon.

"Which way to your bedroom?" I demand.

"Down the hall and to the left."

I slide the glass door open and step inside. Though I know there is a potential threat outside, I don't bother to close it. A slab of wood and a lock is nothing to a supernatural being. If anyone or any being dares interrupt what I am about to do to this woman, they do it at their peril. I will gut any man, woman, or beast who tries to come between us.

I try to keep my steps slow as I make my way through the house. I fail. Marechal doesn't notice the speed at which we move as she reclaims my mouth. Her nails dig into my scalp. Her feet lock at my lower back. Her hard nipples poke through the fabric of her dress.

My eyes are closed as I feel my way through the maze of halls. All of my attention is on Marechal's lips as I revel in the sensation of her lips against mine. How have I spent so many years without kissing? Suckling Marechal's mouth is nearly as good as licking her sweet cunt. I'll need to make a full comparison, noting the pros and cons of each set of her lips. But that will have to be later.

Once in her room, I toss her onto the bed. She

lands with a thud. The fabric of her dress rides up her thighs. My fingers itch to rend the material into strips and tie her down.

I'm distracted when she places her hands over her head and parts her thighs for me, the dark space there beckoning me in. The position of surrender threatens to bring me to my knees.

Here lies the strongest woman I've ever met, and she offers me her submission. No command. No restraints. No deals or ultimatums.

It's a gift. A blessing. A treasure.

I place one knee on the bed. Then the other. Instead of reaching for her, I sink back on my haunches. I have the urge to say a prayer of gratitude.

I have never been a religious man, even though I served during the Inquisition. I tortured men, not for their confessions, but for my own sustenance. I used my skills to get women to confess to crimes they didn't even understand, let alone commit, so that I could make their veins thick with the endorphins of sweet blood.

And for all my sins, Fates has delivered me benediction.

"Are you going to tie me up?"

"No," I whisper. "I'm going to worship your body. Will you hold still for me, *minou*?"

"No." She grins, biting her lip. "I'm going to hold on to you."

She reaches for me then. I swallow hard, holding myself as still as possible. My heart races as she lifts up. My breath quickens as her fingers come slowly towards me. Her palm connects with my jaw, and I gasp. Marechal's flesh against my face is the softest thing I have ever felt in my life.

She cups my face in her hands and kisses me. A small brush of her lips against mine, and I am undone.

She could flay my skin and I would let her. I would welcome the pain. But all her fingertips deliver is pleasure.

"Are you okay?"

She asks because I am shivering. I cannot hide it. I cannot stop it.

Marechal's hand moves to my chest. My heart thumps against its cage, desperate to reach her. I cover her hand with my own and press her palm to feel its beat.

"I want you inside of me," she says.

Does she understand that I need the same thing? With her hand on my chest, Marechal gives me a shove. She is only human, but the nudge knocks me over. My back meets the bed, and she climbs on top of me.

I have never been on the bottom in sex. I have never allowed any woman to place me in this position, not even Domitia. With Marechal on top of me, I reach my hands behind my head, grabbing onto the headboard, preparing to let this woman have her way with me.

25

M*arechal*

I HAVE no idea what I'm doing when I straddle Gaius's hips. I have never been in this position before. I have had power over men in academic situations, in social situations, in business. But I have never been in charge in bed.

I start with what would be practical. For sex to happen, clothes should be off. That is logical.

I grab for the hem of my sundress. The fabric whispers over my thighs as it rises up. Gaius doesn't help. He lies back and watches me, lips pursed as he holds his breath, fists clenched as he withholds his touch.

My fingers shake as I pull the dress over my head. I'm not scared. Or nervous. I want this. I want it so bad, I'm shaking for it.

When I pop the clasp of my bra, my chest heaves a sigh. My nipples point at what they want. Gaius licks his lips, but he doesn't lean in. Is he purposefully denying himself? Does he want me to deny him as he did me? To bring him to the edge again and again before letting him fall over into bliss?

If so, it's too bad. I'm not playing that game. I'm going to run to the edge this time, and jump off. And I'm taking him with me. If my damn fingers can work the buttons of his shirt.

He smirks at my frustration but makes no move to help. With desperate hands, I rip the rest of the shirt open. Knowing Gaius, it cost a small fortune. He only chuckles at its destruction.

I stand when I tug his pants from his legs. With his long legs, it feels like it takes forever for them to pick up the slack and get to the end. He's commando underneath all those layers. I take a moment and simply gaze down at the length of him, as well as the *length* of him.

Am I really about to put all of that inside of me?

"*Viens ici, mon minou.*"

I do. I go to him. I climb back onto my bed. I crawl over his large feet. I scale the length of his thighs. I rise up the range of his chest. When I come face to face with him, I have arrived.

All of the fighting I've done to earn my place in life, all the battles I've waged to be seen and heard, all of my struggles to keep it together—my family, this business, my sense of self—all of it was to get me to this moment with this man.

Looking down at Gaius, I get the sense he feels the same way. We are both open. Our defenses are down. He could gut me in this moment. I could hurt him too.

Cari said Gaius was the glue of his family, the backbone of their business. Like me. We've both left those worries outside the door.

Right now, right here, there's only the two of us. The trust between us is a fragile thread, but it's there. The fibers are strong enough to hold us together in this moment. We both reach for it at the same time. Our fingers come away entwined, our lips together.

The kiss is brutal; thorough. Gaius sips at my soul. His tongue penetrates so deeply that I can feel the pulls deep in my core. Can I orgasm just from his kiss? I bet he could make me.

I need more of him than just his tongue or his hands. I want that big cock inside of me. His hard length tickles my belly button. The tip is giving me a wet kiss of its own.

I lift my hips, angling to get the long rod between my thighs. I have to rise all the way up on my knees to accomplish the feat. Once his cock is inside me and he has his tongue down my throat, I wonder if the two would meet?

I position his head between my intimate curls. I'm so wet with excitement that the thick head slips easily inside me. The launch was the easy part. The landing is not so much bumpy as it is long. I won't get to see if his tongue and dick are long enough to meet inside me because he breaks the kiss.

"*Merde*," Gaius hisses.

His hands halt my descent. His fingers dig into my hips as he breathes hard.

I'm breathing hard, too, but it's because I want more. I want all of him. I wriggle my hips for my access but he curses again.

"I just forgot what this feels like," he says. "I haven't been inside a woman in centuries."

"What?"

His words make no sense. He doesn't bother

explaining them. Instead, he claims my mouth again and I forget what he said.

I let out a long sigh when he is fully seated in me. I can feel him everywhere. In the curl of my toes. In the scrape of my nipples against his chest. Underneath my fingernails, which make half-moons in his back.

I could stay like this all night; Gaius filling me up to my eyelids. It's the first time in my life that I've known contentment. But the throbbing length inside me wants movement, which brings me back to my initial conundrum.

I have no idea what I'm doing when I straddle Gaius's hips.

The control he'd lent me was short-lived. It ran out the moment I put the tip in. His hands lift my hips. I moan in protest as his hardness recedes. I scream in surrender as he thrusts into me.

One hand is a piston on my ass, pumping me up and down his shaft. With the other, he rubs my clit in light, leisurely circles that are at odds with his hard thrusts. The polar sensations pull me apart, and I'm coming before my mind understands what's happening.

The orgasms Gaius had given me before this were with his fingers, with his tongue, with the bristles of a paintbrush. This time, his firm mass is inside of me. My muscles clench around solid steel, and my entire being rings like I am a bell.

Still pumping in and out of me, Gaius shoves one, then two fingers inside me. There should be no room, but he makes it so. His cock thrusts, then his fingers. Into the impossibly full space, he forces a third digit. It hooks up, hitting a bundle of nerves at the front of my sex.

I'm trembling, shaking, unintelligible when I come next.

My upper body collapses down atop him. He lies back with me in his arms, but he doesn't miss a single thrust. His fingers leave my quaking pussy and circle round to my ass. Gaius's seeking fingers rub at the puckered hole there.

He can't be thinking... and then he does. He presses a finger into my asshole.

His cock fills my channel. His tongue thrusts into my mouth. His finger pumps into my ass. I am invaded, and again, I surrender.

This time when I come, Gaius halts his thrusts. I am sitting on his cock, on his finger, filled to the brim as I moan into his mouth and he swallows down my cries.

But he is not done. When my shivers ease, Gaius

lifts me off his cock. Like my hips are nothing more than a serving dish, he sets my pussy up to his face. Parting the swollen lips between my thighs, he sets my clit on his tongue as though it were an *amuse-bouche*. His eyes never leaving me, he laves at me until I come again.

Before I come down, he's shifted me back to his cock.

"Touch yourself," he commands.

I do as I'm told. My fingers glide over my sex, feeling the softness of my flesh and the hard ridges of his.

His hands are cupping my ass, making me thrust against him, harder. Harder. My hips buck out of control. I am mindless, my body moving out of instinct.

Gaius yanks my hands away. Without my palm against this chest for balance, I fall into him. This is what he wanted.

He crushes me to his chest. He wraps my arms behind my back, holding them there in a vice. Then he bucks into me, even harder.

His free hand goes to my hair. He grabs fistfuls and tugs my head back, exposing my neck as he bucks into me. The slapping of his hips, of his dick into my welcoming wetness, is music in my ears. That, and my cries of mindless pleasure.

I have nothing to hold on to. He has me trapped on top of him. Here I thought I would take control of the situation, but this man has taken control of me entirely. If there was more of myself that I could give to him, I'd hand it over with a *merci beaucoup*.

And still, he's thrusting into me. His pumping hasn't let up. Not once. Not even now as I come again.

My entire body seizes around him. I come so hard that I wonder if I've died. The trembling never stops, not even when I fall limp onto the bed.

My back goes against the cushion of the bed. Gaius climbs on top of me. I want to reach out to him, to hold him to me. But I can't move a muscle.

He parts my thighs, bringing his hips between mine. I feel him enter me. The broadness of his cock is not one that could ever be ignored, no matter how spent I am.

He slides in and out of me. Slower now. Controlled. But deeper. It's as though he's trying to get to my heart through my pussy. I wish I could open wider for him. I wish I could clear the path of every organ and blood vessel that was in the way.

I can only open my eyes and gaze up at him. He

looks like a man lost. Not lost in a place. It's clear he knows where he is. He just seems lost as to how to get where he's going.

I find the strength to lift my hand to his cheek. I caress his strong jaw. Gaius closes his eyes. The most exquisite look of pleasure and pain crosses his features as he shouts a guttural cry. His body bucks into mine. I realize then, it's the first time he's come all night. He collapses down onto me, and allows me to hold him in my arms.

26

___

G *aius*

"I can't feel my toes."

Marechal might not be able to feel her toes, but I can. Her warm flesh rubs up and down the inside of my calf. Instead of pulling away from the intimate touch, I roll into her, needing to feel more of her against me.

"You're still speaking," I say. "Which means I haven't done my job properly."

"Oh, no." Her eyes go wide with shock but also

desire. "I can not have another orgasm. My body can't take it."

I rise up on one elbow, gazing down at her. She is bare and bruised. Her lips are red from my kisses, her cunt swollen from my thrusts. "Are you telling me no, *minou*?"

She gulps. "Gaius..."

My dick stirs again. I've fucked her for hours until she went limp, and then I right alongside her. Yet, here I am again, getting hard for her. "I think I'm going to fuck you until you pass out."

I reach for her. For a woman who has been thoroughly fucked, she moves a little too fast for my liking. I could easily catch her, but where would the fun be in that? She giggles when I do catch her. The sound is a delight to my black soul.

"Is that your kink?" she says from within the cage of my arms. The amusement in her eyes shifts and shines brighter. "You liked it when I was so blissed out that I couldn't move. That's when you came."

I let out a slow sigh. Already, I've bared more than I am comfortable to this woman. She still claws for more. Her hand comes to rest on my cheek. I flinch at her touch, but only slightly. Of course, she catches the movement. But being Marechal, she comes at it from a different angle.

"Cari said you take care of your brothers. Who takes care of you?"

"The same person who takes care of all your needs in the small cracks of time you give to yourself."

The light in her eyes dims as it turns inward. I want to take it back. I want to be the one who causes her to be light. I want to put her on my care list—possibly even above the care of my brothers.

No, not possibly. Definitely above the care of my brothers. I want to take every care from this woman and make it my own so that she doesn't have a single burden. I want her to know that my back is strong enough to bear everything she can give me, and then some.

"Do you think, maybe, we could take care of each other?" Marechal's fingers glide down my chin.

I hadn't thought of that. I hadn't considered that maybe she would offer to carry some of my load. No one has ever done that for me.

If ever anyone could handle all that I am, it would be Marechal Durand. But to make that happen, I would have to take her life and give her a new one. Am I ready for that?

The sun will be up in a few hours. The thought of being parted from her is an anathema in my chest.

I want her with me when it's light, to keep her safe from the brightness.

My brothers think I'm falling in love with this woman. I don't know about that. I've seen the expression in art, heard about it in songs, read about it in poetry. In real life? I don't know what it means.

All I know is I want to protect this woman. I want to ease her burdens. I want to give her pleasure. I want her to turn to me in her time of need. And... it would be nice if perhaps I could turn to her if ever I needed to, as well.

It's too much to think about. It's too heavy to deal with. Right now, I just want to make her moan. I just want to lose myself in her in the time I have left before sunrise. I just want to sink my fangs into her and sate my thirst.

It's been days since I've eaten. Bagged blood held no appeal. Another woman wasn't even on the table. I just want her.

So, I take her.

I duck my head out of her gentle caress. With rough hands, I flip Marechal onto her back. After a gasp of surprise, she lets out a delighted scream.

I part her thighs. I can smell the blood pumping in her femoral artery. I'll give her another orgasm and then take a quick drink. I know hers will be the sweetest blood I've ever drunk. Holding my aching fangs at bay, I've dipped my head to begin my attack when the bedroom door bangs open.

I don't think. I react. I fly from the bed and have the intruder in my clutches in a blink. My fangs are bared. My claws are in his neck.

"Gaius, no."

Marechal's voice is a faint plea in my ears. But the rage flowing through me is too loud. Tiny points of blood trickle down my victim's neck from the indents of my nails. My nostrils flare as I note that his blood smells similar to Marechal's. His wide eyes are the same dark plum color as her own.

Arneis Durand gasps as he tears at my hand around his throat. A slight fog from his eyes is clearing even as I choke the life out of him. The fog is one I put there myself, just a few days ago, when I wiped his mind of the memory of the car crash he'd been in with Cari. And then of Domitia drinking his blood. And also of Hadrian feeding Arneis his vampiric blood to save the man's life.

As Arneis stares at me, terror in his eyes, all those sealed memories are coming unlocked. I could put him in thrall again, willing him to forget the last

five seconds. But memory wiping is a delicate business. And there's the matter of his sister scrambling
behind us.

"Gaius, let him go."

I let him down. Arneis wobbles as his feet touch
the ground. His eyes blink rapidly, trying to focus.
And then his entire body slumps to the ground.

Marechal rushes past me. She is wrapped in
bedsheets as she bends over her brother. "Arnei? Are
you okay?"

Arneis closes his eyes and gulps down lungfuls
of air. When he opens them again he continues to
blink rapidly, trying to pull his thoughts into focus.

"What did you do to him?" Marechal's gaze turns
to me. Her tone is accusatory.

"I thought he was an attacker," I say. "He
burst in."

"This is his home," she says, running her hands
over her brother's face just as she had done mine
moments ago. "*Mon ami*, look at me. Can you
breathe?"

He's breathing fine. He'll be fine. It's his memories I worry about.

Arneis's gaze locks on his sister, then shifts and
focuses on me. "You monster," he whispers.

And there it is. Arneis's memories are unlocked.

I'm about to be shoved out of the supernatural closet before I'm ready.

I'll have to fess up to Marechal, which has consequences I'm not sure I'm ready for. Or I'll have to wipe both their minds, which I know I'm not prepared to do.

I don't want Marechal to forget a single second of what we shared. Those memories are too precious, and I don't want to hold them alone. I want her to carry them with me. On into the morning, and into tomorrow night. Maybe forever.

"Arneis, you can't just barge into my room like this."

The sound of bossy Marechal makes my dick hard again. I want to dare her to speak to me like that. Just so I can dole out the consequences on that perfect ass.

"I thought he was hurting you," Arneis says. "Like he hurt Cari."

"Cari's fine," I say. "And Marechal was enjoying what I was doing to her before you interrupted."

"Don't help." Marechal holds a finger up at me, and my fangs throb.

Arneis shakes his head. Perhaps trying to clear it? Perhaps trying to shake more memories into view? "They took her from us. I was driving her away from them, and then she dropped out of the sky and took her from us."

Arneis points an accusatory finger at me. But the finger is shaky. The fear in his eyes tells me it's not my face he's seeing. It's Domitia's. I'm a centuries-old supernatural being, and just the thought of her stops my dead heart.

"Gaius, why don't you go?"

Me? Go? As in leave Marechal? That is the last thing I'm going to do.

"My brother is still having trouble from the accident. He hit his head, and... concussions are hard."

Arneis holds his head in his hand. It's not a concussion that's causing the confusion.

"I'll stay," I say.

Marechal shakes her head as she stands. She places her hand on my chest. Had she been another woman, I would've caught her wrist and then turned her over my knee for daring to take such a liberty. But my heart leaps at her touch and I step closer to her.

"This is a family matter."

She gives my chest a gentle shove. I nearly fall down as the impact hits me. No blood is drawn because her nails don't scratch my skin. Her palm is flat, not balled into a fist as the brunt of her flesh hits me soft in the chest. Her words are a slap in the face, harsher than any blow Domitia ever doled out.

I have let this woman touch the darkest parts of me. I have let her reach inside of me. I have lain down all of my defenses at her feet. And she is turning her back on me and reaching out for another.

Marechal goes back down on her knees. She hovers over her brother, giving him all of her care. Brushing Arneis's hair from his forehead, she coos soothing words to him.

Me, she's forgotten. Put aside, because I am not her family. I am not first on her list.

My jaw won't work to form words, so I turn. I grab my pants on the way out, not bothering with shoes or a shirt. I need a drink, a sweet drink from a willing victim. I need to tie someone down and flog her until she is dripping, begging. Needing me. Wanting only me. Knowing that only I can provide the release she needs.

And when I'm done with her, I'll leave her to someone else for aftercare. I'll crawl under my bed and sleep alone. Shut myself inside my crypt where I am safe, and no one can touch me.

I step out into the night. If I want to get to Club

Toxic, I'll need to move fast. The sun is only a few hours away, which doesn't leave much time to play.

I turn to do just that but don't get far. The air leaves my lungs. Something has come down hard on my head. I lose my footing and go down to my knees. Then I feel a second strike, and all goes black.

27

M *arechal*

THE QUIET SNICK of the door reverberates in my ears. Every part of me wants to chase after Gaius. To grab hold of his hands, which had balled into two tight fists. To brush my lips against his mouth, which had compressed into a thin line. To wrap my arms around his body, which had stiffened and closed off.

All the walls we'd torn down between us moments ago were just bricked over in the blink of an eye. My dismissal hurt him. But Gaius's hurt feelings can wait until the morning. Right now, my brother is in crisis.

"There's something wrong about all of this," Arneis says.

His knees are pulled into his chest. His arms are wrapped tightly around them. He rocks his torso in the way he only ever did as a child, soon after our mother passed.

"I'm missing something, Mare."

Like me, Arneis has always been a rock. He looks at a problem, ingests the facts, and spits out a logical solution. With his analytical, straightforward thinking, he's never been perceptive enough to see the curveballs coming his way.

"We have to find Cari," he adds.

I pull the cover tighter around me as I sit next to my brother. "Cari is fine, Arnei. I talked to her earlier today. She's with Hadrian."

Arneis shakes his head, violently, as though there are bees buzzing around in his head. My hand was on his shoulder. I snatch it out of the way as his body trembles.

"She's not safe. He's going to bite her."

"Arneis, you're not making sense."

"I'm trying," he shouts. "I'm trying to remember."

My brother's eyes are haunted as he looks up at

me. His hands go to his head. He rubs at his temples as though trying to loosen the knot that has a hold on him.

"They're after me." His voice is a whisper. His eyes are wide, irises darting back and forth between the corners of his eyes. "I think they have her."

"Who are you talking about?"

"Lucius Frangelico."

That's the name of the man who was trying to buy the vineyard before the Serranos stepped in. I don't know much about Frangelico, except that he is probably richer than god and owns an exclusive club downtown.

"You don't know what they get up to in that club. They get deliveries from a bloodmobile. The Serranos go there. I saw them."

That catches my attention. Arneis is not a club-goer. As a kid, he preferred dress pants to jeans, and a tie to any sport's jersey.

"Arneis, you're not making any sense. The doctor's said you suffered a concussion from the accident—"

"It wasn't a concussion. It was the white-haired woman." His gaze is far away, but it's not hazy. He looks clear-eyed, like he's watching a scene play out in his mind. "She had sharp teeth. She bit me. She took Cari."

My throat is too raw to speak. My eyes sting with unshed tears. I'm used to taking care of my sick siblings. But no chicken noodle soup, or aspirin, or kissing of booboos, is going to fix this.

Arneis rubs at his neck. There are two raised bumps there, right over the jugular. But those could easily be bug bites.

"When I came to, Hadrian was pressing his wrist to my mouth. He was feeding me his blood."

"Arneis, that's enough." I tug at his arm to pull him up. But he won't budge.

"And then Gaius stared into my eyes. He told me to forget, and I did."

Arneis's gaze focuses on me. His dark eyes are clear, as clear as when he's doing a math problem in his head and arrives at the answer without the aid of a calculator.

"He was trying to do it again just now. I could feel him in my mind, Marechal."

His voice is desperate now. He grips my shoulders with both his hands. His hold on me is painful, but nowhere near as bad as the pain I feel as I watch my little brother lose his mind.

"It wasn't an accident," says Arneis. "I went to get

Cari. We were driving. And then this woman came out of nowhere. She had fangs. She bit me. Then she took Cari."

"Cari is fine," I say as calmly as I can. "I'll call her so you can talk to her yourself."

But after I dial her number, the phone just rings and rings. I pull up Hadrian's number and get the same result. They're newlyweds and it's the middle of the night. What should I expect? But I need Arneis to see that there is no truth to what he's made up in his mind.

White-haired women falling from the sky and biting him. Hadrian feeding him blood. Gaius wiping his mind. It's all a result of his head injury. I'd rather convince my brother myself than have him see a doctor, as that would certainly ruin his career as a public servant.

The next number I dial is Gaius's. It hasn't been long enough for him to get from my place to his. Maybe he can turn around and come back.

I shouldn't have sent him away in the first place. This isn't a problem I know how to handle. And I don't want to handle it on my own.

Gaius's phone rings in the ear I have pressed to the phone. Then it rings again, loud and clear in my other ear. I pull my phone away and the ringing continues. I spy Gaius's phone on the floor where he left his ruined shirt.

I bend down to pick up the phone. There are two alerts on the screen. One is a missed call from me. The other is a text from Hadrian.

Cari and I are playing in the cellar. Don't come knocking.

The cellar? The one with the sex toys hanging on the wall and spanking apparatus in the center? The one sitting out back of the Serrano main house?

"Arneis, get up. We're going to pay a visit to our new in-laws."

28

———

G*aius*

CONTRARY TO POPULAR BELIEF, vampires do get headaches. There's nothing wrong with our nerve endings. All of our senses are simply enhanced. We can feel the same pain as humans, especially if doled out by a weapon of mass destruction, or another supernatural creature.

There are claw marks next to the bump at the base of my skull. They're both healing rapidly, but sting as my body regenerates the torn flesh. I'm healing a little slower than usual since I skipped yesterday's meal and barely ate the day before that. So the throb at the base of my skull feels like a freight train is ramming into it, shifting into reverse, backing up, and ramming it again.

Were I not so thirsty, it wouldn't be so bad. During my time with Domitia, this would've been considered foreplay. She would've made sure I was well fed, all so that she could make the pain last longer.

My only care is for Marechal. I can still smell her on me. But I don't smell her in here. The fact that she is safe eases my worries. Which takes my mind back to the pain.

It takes a long moment for the blackness to recede. It takes my eyes a few seconds more before my surroundings become clear. Overhead, there is an open shaft that lets in the moonlight. But there isn't much to see.

I smell rich earth, but with an underlying mustiness of mold. The walls are cold. Hard. Rock.

I'm in a cave. One that's deep underground. If I inhale deeply enough, I can smell berries. Not the tart berries of the Durand vineyard. I smell the unmistakable sweet reds of the Serrano grapes.

I'm back on my land. But I'm not in my home. I'm somewhere deep underneath it, in the caves my brothers and I explored when we first came here. When we came here months ago, we caught no whiff of shifters. Now the place reeks of cat.

Just great. When the others learn I was taken down by a pack of felines, I will never hear the end of it.

A movement to the side instantly clears my head of any residual pain. It looks like the big kitties have come out to play. Eyes flash at me in the darkness of the cave.

There is an open alcove. Three males stand in the doorway. They are large, with black hair and brown skin. I don't see any of the female shifters from the vineyard, but I can smell them nearby.

The women had appeared docile in the vineyard. I should've known better. As a vampire, I am higher up on the food chain than their species, but they are natural predators. Their four-legged ancestors roamed these lands long before humans stood to walk on two feet.

"You know you are breaking the peace treaty," I say, aiming for diplomacy. "Lucius Frangelico has signed an accord with the shifters of this territory."

"We are not under Frangelico's thumb. Or that dog, Garrett Green."

I should've guessed that. The vineyard is just out

of Frangelico's territory. And I should have known that wolf shifters and cat shifters wouldn't mix. But it was worth a try. "What do you want?"

"This land is ours," says the larger one. He wears his hair in two long braids that trail over his shoulders. His features are so fine that he might be mistaken for a girl if it weren't for his bare chest and bulging biceps.

"I have a deed that says otherwise."

"Words on paper mean nothing to us." Mr. Pippi Longstocking takes a step into the cave. "Our forefathers lived on this land long before your blood was poisoned by your maker."

I take my time coming to my feet, making certain not to make any sudden moves. There still might be a way to get out of this without bloodshed.

Shifters are strong. So are vampires. My ability to trace would even my odds despite the unfair number of males before me. But I don't know these caves, and I have a feeling they're hiding their numbers. I can smell more bodies outside the door. More testosterone that's eager for a fight.

"Sounds like something you fellas are going to have to take up with the government."

Longstocking snorts at that. The other two give me a hard stare. I can't blame them. The US government gave Native Americans a raw deal at every turn. The Spanish regents and church ordered the Inquisition. In all my centuries, I've never met a governing body that actually had what was best for the people in mind.

The government won't help in this matter. Neither will documents or deeds. This is a supernatural problem.

"You're the reason my grapes aren't growing," I say.

Longstocking shakes his head. "No, that's the prophecy."

This night just keeps getting better. The reason I like the wine business so much is because it doesn't deal with any magical bullshit. It's science. Filled with predictable variables that I can control. Unlike foretelling and soothsaying.

I'd rather deal with the church. At least then I know any evildoing could always be linked back to the desires of wicked men out to grab power or money. Prophecies? Those are beyond this realm, and rarely bring anything good.

"What prophecy?"

He doesn't answer. He steps back. There is a loud, cranking groan as the door of the alcove is shut. Then a clank as a lock slams into place.

Great. I'm locked in an underground cave surrounded by a bunch of jaguar shifters. A perfect ending to a perfect night. Except the night isn't over, and it will be soon.

Up above, I can see the moon in the shaft of the cave's opening. The white orb is slowly sinking down the horizon. In just a couple of hours, it will descend. And the sun will rise.

"Uh oh, did the big bad vampire forget his sunshades?"

The voice comes from the other side of the cave. There is a woman sitting on a small mattress on the floor. She's dressed in a thin shift that leaves nothing to the imagination. She lies back with her arms crossed behind her head, her painted toes hanging off the bedding.

Exactly what kind of prophecy is going on here?

29

M *arechal*

I PULL up to the Serrano vineyard less than ten minutes after leaving home. The drive should've taken over twenty, but my foot never left the gas.

I will always go full speed ahead with anything to do with my family, be they in need, or lying through their teeth.

I can't believe Cari lied to me. She's kept things from me before. But never a bold-faced, *I'm out of the country on my honeymoon, not hiding out in my husband's sex cellar* lie.

When I get hold of my little sister, I'll... what? Berate her for wanting to have a little private fun with her new husband?

No, I won't do that. I'm not angry anymore. I'm filled with worry and uncertainty. Cari likely has her reasons for keeping me in the dark about her whereabouts. But I can't grasp what's going on with my brother.

In the passenger seat, Arneis is white-knuckling the seat belt. I should have thought about his nerves. He's just survived an accident. And our father died in one last year.

But I can't think of everyone else right now. I need him to see Cari for himself. To see that she is healthy and whole and without fangs.

Vampires? Where could he have gotten such an idea? Arneis was never one for fantasy novels. I can't remember him reading fiction outside of school-work. He prefers historical biographies, social treatises, and political speeches throughout the ages with annotated commentary. Vampires are not in his wheelhouse.

I can't have this getting out. If he begins spouting stories about vampires out in polite society, he will be booted out of public office at sunrise. But Arneis is a logical man. Once I show him Cari, once he sits down and talks with Hadrian and Gaius, everything will click back into place in his head. He'll see the error of his muddled thoughts. He has to. The alternative would be to turn to doctors, and that would likely get leaked to the media.

All is quiet when we pull through the gates of the Serrano vineyard. I see Gaius's car in the driveway. Good, he's here. I grab his phone. His shirt is still back at my place, now tucked in my top dresser drawer. It's not likely he'll wear it again, but I have designs on making it my new nightie. Though I would prefer to sleep in his arms.

I eye the wine cellar off to the side of the house. If my sister is in there, she is likely naked and in the throes of passion. Not necessarily something I want to see. Definitely not something that will help her older brother's psyche. So, I turn to the house.

I raise my fist to knock. A niggling at the nape of my neck urges me to try the knob. Unballing my fist, I wrap my fingers around the cool metal, and it gives.

I expect the hinges to creak. They don't. The door whispers open, allowing us entry.

"Wait." Arneis grabs my forearm. "Don't we have to be invited inside?"

"That's a rule for vampires; they have to be invited into a human's home. We're not—" I clamp my mouth shut and pinch the bridge of my nose. I'm so tired that I nearly bought into this nonsense. After letting out a gush of a sigh, I proceed inside.

"Gaius?" I call into the dark hall.

Feeling along the wall, I don't find any switches for light fixtures. I can navigate my own home in the dark, having lived there all my life. But I am instantly lost in this maze of halls and rooms that not even the moonlight penetrates.

I take another step forward and bump into a hard wall. The wall reaches out and grabs my arm. I scream.

Light floods the room, and the wall of flesh comes into view. Virius has a hand under my armpit. He's holding me up. In front of me are a set of stairs that lead outside. One more step, and I would've fallen down them and broken my neck.

From behind me, Arneis lets loose a battle cry. He charges Virius. Arneis is a big man, but Virius is broad. My brother collides into the wall that is Virius and falls back on his ass. His head thuds against the floor, likely causing another concussion.

I jerk free of Virius's hold to join my brother on the floor. Arneis groans as he rubs his head.

Virius gazes down at the two of us, his head

cocked to the side as he studies us. "Gaius isn't here. I thought he was with you."

"He left my place nearly an hour ago," I say as I help Arneis to sit up. "His car is out front."

"He didn't drive to your place. He walked there."

My gaze swings from my brother up to Virius. "He walked? I live over ten miles away."

Virius shrugs. I note the man is wearing cowboy chaps and a t-shirt with a Native American in a headdress on it. The mismatch of cultural appropriation gives me pause... until I see what he has in his hand.

"I told you." Arneis raises a shaky finger, pointing at the object in Virius's hand. "Vampires."

Virius looks down, then he curses. "Great, now Cari will be pissed at me. She didn't want you two to know."

I stare, stunned, as Virius lifts the bag of blood to his mouth. His sharp teeth gleam in the moonlight. He punctures a hole at the top of the bag and then takes a pull like he's a kid sipping from a Capri Sun juice pouch.

I can't decide if I should scream out of fear, or gag out of disgust. My mind is so scrambled that I can't make a move. I can only stare as Virius drains the bag dry and then swipes the back of his hand over his mouth.

"You'll have to wait for Gaius to get home, or for Hadrian to come out of the dungeon with Cari. I'm shite at mind wiping. I might take everything, and then Cari will be really pissed. Luckily, she's not the type to bind my balls. At least, she hasn't tried yet."

That's all I need to hear. I don't know exactly what it is that I just saw. What I do know is that I need to get my brother up and away from this man. Then I need to find my sister, and get her out of this nuthouse.

I manage to get Arneis to his feet. Virius doesn't make a move towards us. He simply watches as we snake around him to the stairs that lead outside. Once the cool night air hits my face, I tell Arneis to run. But my foot hits the ground wrong and I go down.

I reach out to brace my fall. I'm able to protect my face, but my hands bear the brunt. The sharp edge of a rock slices into the flesh of my palm. The pain shoots through me and my knee goes down, catching another rock.

I roll over to find Virius looking down at me. The man's nose twitches as he looks at the blood. His white fangs flash in the dark night.

"Don't worry; I already ate." Virius holds up the empty pouch as evidence, but something else moves in the night.

I hear the crash of a door being swung open, then a high-pitched scream, followed by a low growl. From the cellar at the back of the house, I catch a blur of hair and limbs.

Cari.

The pain in my hands and knee are forgotten as my sister comes into view. I lift my arms, wanting to reach out her, to hold her in my arms. But there's something chasing her; something big and fast.

It's nearly on her. It grabs hold of her ankle, and they both go down. As they roll on the ground, I see Cari's pursuer is Hadrian.

They roll in the grass. Not with the passion of lovers, but with the aggression of two individuals at odds.

Cari slips free of Hadrian's hold and she is up, running towards me again. Her lips pull back from her teeth, revealing sharp white fangs.

"Cari, no."

My sister's fangs flash at me. There is no recognition in her eyes. Her gaze is fixed on the blood dripping from my outstretched hand.

30

———————

G*aius*

THE WOMAN STEPS into the moonlight. By all accounts, she is breathtaking, with striking features. Her skin is a few shades darker than Marechal's. Her hair is a curtain of ebony. Her eyes are hazel, not the dark plum of a Sémillion grape. They flash at me, revealing her shifter nature.

A few days ago, I would've been curious to know what color her nipples were, what shade of red her cunt was, how long she would last at the edge of my cat o'nine tail whip.

I'm not interested in the answer to any of those queries. All I can think about is how to get out of the hell I am in. My gaze turns skyward.

"You're not going to make that climb," she says, coming to stand next to me.

She's small. But the way she holds herself makes me feel as though she's looking down her nose at me. I get the sense that she is a leader. So why is she the one trapped in here with me?

"My name is Gaius Serrano."

"I know who you are."

"Might I know the pleasure of your name?"

"Ixazaluoh."

She cocks her head to the side. It's a clear challenge. Even with my slick tongue, I can't repeat that grouping of consonants and vowels.

"Thought so," she scoffs. "You may call me Zahara."

"Zahara, you want to tell me what I'm doing here? What is this prophecy?"

"It has nothing to do with you. Those idiots brought the wrong man." She rubs her hands over her forehead. The lines there don't smooth under her touch; they remain creased, as if she carries the weight of the world there.

"Fine," I say. "Let's just tell them that and then they can let me go."

Zahara drops her hand and she cocks her head to the other side. The chit looks like she only just entered her twenties. I have centuries on her, but I'm left feeling as though my suggestion is foolish.

"That's not the plan," she says.

"Want to clue me in on what the plan is? I may be able to help."

Again, she scoffs, the lines on her face making deeper grooves. "Why would I send a man to do a woman's job? What I need from you is to get on the bed."

I look at the dusty mattress on the ground, then back at her. Is she expecting me to fuck her? It would make sense. Talk of a prophecy. Cursed lands. She is likely the virginal sacrifice. Too bad my dick had no desire to get it up for anyone but Marechal.

"I'm not going to sleep with you."

Zahara snorts as she looks me up and down, obviously finding me wanting. "That's rich, coming from you. Your reputation has reached even as far as Central America, Lord of the Lash."

I wince at the use of the moniker. When I open my mouth, Zahara holds up her hand to indicate she's not done talking.

"Marechal Durand is one of the good ones. She deserves better than a player like you."

"She not good; she's the best. I'm a better man because of her. I want to be everything that woman needs. So help me get back to her."

Zahara studies me again. I'm not certain if this perusal has earned me a reassessment.

"The only way back to your girlfriend is through me." She waves her hands over her barely covered private area. "However, I have no intention of being some exotic sacrifice to a white man. This isn't Disney's Pocahontas."

"I'm not white. I'm from Gaul."

She frowns as though that historical detail matters. "We're going to pretend we're doing the deed."

"You mean have sex?"

The grooves dig further into her forehead as she sighs. "Please let there be some brain cells in that pretty little head of yours. We..." she points between the two of us, "are not getting horizontal. You're not the right one. If we have sex, it won't break the curse."

There is a part of me that wants to understand the curse and the prophecy that will break it. This business has been my life for centuries, I don't want it to fail. But a larger part of me needs to be free of this place and get back to Marechal. She is all that I can see of my future. If I follow along with Zahara's plan, she could get me closer to the bigger goal. Then, once we're free, I can find out more about the mystical mayhem going on.

"We're going to act like it," she's saying. "We're going to make sex noises, rumple the sheets, make it believable. You know; a little oohhh and ahhh."

"Have you ever even had sex?" I ask. Her cries are the most unenthusiastic I've ever heard. Whatever her future, it won't be in the porn industry.

My critique sobers her up. Her eyes flash at me. The cat in her is ready to come out, claws blazing.

"My hymen is my business. A woman's virginity is not a prize. Maybe I fucked all of Central America. Maybe I'm saving it for a special man. But that man is not you. So get your mind out of my panties."

"You're the one who's miming fake sex and lame orgasms. I give mind-blowing sex and screaming orgasms, if you want to know." It's a point of professional pride. Even though I'm turning in my membership card at Club Toxic, I still have a reputation to protect.

"I don't want to know," Zahara hisses. "I don't

need to know. We just need to make those males out there believe."

"And then they'll let us out?"

Zahara bites her lip, not meeting my gaze. "They'll let me out. You, they'll try to kill."

"Right. I'm not exactly on board with your plan."

"That's why we'll need to act fast." She pulls a dagger from under the mattress. "My sisters will be at the ready once I give the signal."

"You would kill your own people?"

"The men out there are not my people. All they want is this land. And they're going to try and use my womb to get it."

"Your womb?" So this prophecy is a step beyond virginal sacrifice. It requires the birth of a child as well. "You know vampires can't have children?"

"Shows how much you know."

Zahara steps onto the bed and begins to jump up and down while making grunting and groaning noises. I stare, aghast. It's the worse porno I've ever witnessed in my life. And I am its costar.

31

———

Marechal

WHEN CARI WAS TEETHING, she was a nightmare. She would wail, her little mouth open wide as those first teeth broke her swollen gums and pushed through. Once the first couple were through, her toothy smile could brighten anyone's day.

Those teeth are flashing at me now. Fear should stab my heart. Horror should pierce my consciousness. My beautiful, bright baby sister has become a monster. The little girl I've cared for all her life looms over me, preparing to take my life from me.

Behind me, Arneis bellows. It is a gut-wrenching demand for Cari to stop. An agonizing cry for her to come to recognize her sister, her family.

My senses sharpen as my life flashes before my eyes. The smell of dying berries is the first thing that penetrates my consciousness. I see Arnei and Cari barefoot as they stomp grapes in a barrel, while I tinker with the valve that collects the juices. I hear Arneis reciting a speech for a student election while Cari watches cartoons. Sound is all around me but my gaze is focused in the lens of my microscope. In another memory, I'm at dinner with my brother and sister, but my thoughts are on my wine glass which holds a competitor's blend. I can't remember a single word of what my siblings said that night, but I can remember the notes of the wine.

I have always been there for my siblings. What I haven't been is present, in the moment, tuned in to them. Because I didn't know how. It was Gaius who taught me that. He just had to tie me down to do it.

Cari has slipped Hadrian's grasp. She's dodged around Virius, faster than my human eyes could perceive. And now she's on me.

My back impacts the ground hard. I wince. I open my eyes to see my sister above me.

Her eyes are glowing with an otherworldly light.

Her teeth gleam in the moon's glow. I think back to that baby and her first teeth. She'd bitten me then. I'd scowled at her. But then she'd laughed, and I'd forgiven her.

This time, I don't think I'll survive my sister's bite. She's a vampire. I don't understand how this can be. But it is.

She is a creature of the night. So is her husband, whose eyes are also shining bright. So is Virius, with a dribble of pouch blood on his chin. So must be Gaius.

I should feel powerless at this moment. I don't. All I feel is the need to protect my family, like always. To make sure they have everything that they might need in this world. And if that need is my blood, then so be it.

I reach my bloody hand up to Cari's face. Her nose twitches as I run my fingertips over her cheek. Her lips quiver as I cup her chin in my palm.

She leans into my hand and closes her eyes. Her nostrils flare as the blood trickles down the fleshy part of my palm. Cari's fangs protrude further from her gums.

She doesn't cry as she did as a teething baby. She doesn't smile, either, but I can't help noticing that she is just as beautiful and bright now as when she was a tiny thing in my arms. And then she is flying off me.

Hadrian has her in his arms. He turns her so that she is caught against his chest. He steps back from me, but I can hear Cari crying.

That's what guts me. Not the knowledge that my vampire sister was about to rip out my throat. The sound of her torment that she'd nearly done it.

"I almost did it," Cari whimpers.

"But you didn't," Hadrian soothes. "You are so strong. My strong girl."

Hadrian strokes her hair, petting her as though she were a pet. His hold on her is absolute, like she is a precious gem that he will never be parted from.

I sit up, the world spinning a bit as I do. I look for my brother, who is trying to break out from behind the wall of Virius's outstretched arms. I look back to my sister, whose shoulders shake with tearful misery.

"Cari?"

She doesn't raise her head. She won't look at me.

"Cari, I'm okay. You didn't hurt me."

I place my feet underneath me but am still a bit wobbly from my multiple falls. Virius comes to me. He rips his shirt up and bandages my hand.

"Look, Cari." I hold up my covered hand. "It's all gone. I'm fine."

Her shoulders stop shaking. She tucks her chin to her chest. She doesn't look directly at me. I can only see her profile.

"Why didn't you tell me?" I ask.

"Tell you what?" She sniffles. "That I died and came back a vampire? I figured you'd get pissed."

"I am pissed." I turn my gaze to Hadrian. "You didn't even ask me for her hand, yet you saw fit to take her life."

At least the man—scratch that. At least the vampire has the good sense to look cowed. I may have just had the near-death epiphany that I needed to to be more present for my family. But that doesn't mean I'll back down in the bossiness level.

"Hadrian, you and I are going to have a talk about that," I say.

Cari lifts her head then. She gives Hadrian the smirk she used to give Arneis when they were in trouble and knew a punishment from their big sister was coming.

"You're taking this all very well, Mare," says Cari.

No. I am in shock—likely with a heavy helping of denial. Vampires are real. What next? Will the

Easter Bunny rise up on its haunches and walk over with a basket of bunny eggs?

"We're going to all have a sit down and talk about this over breakfast," I say.

"Um, Mare," says Cari, fully facing me now as she wipes the tears away. "We don't do sun. Allergy."

Right. Looks like my family as well as the vineyard will be switching to a nocturnal schedule. My family has now doubled in size. And the males now outnumber the females. That will be different.

"So, bedtime soon for you three," I say, looking at the moon as it dips lower in the sky. "Where is Gaius?"

"He's not with you?" asks Hadrian.

"He left when Arneis came. That was over an hour ago. I assumed he was coming home."

"He's here." Virius's nose is lifted to the sky, like a bloodhound catching a scent.

"He's not in the house," says Cari, her gaze scanning the darkened house as though she can see all.

"Viri is right," says Hadrian. "He's here. On the property. But his scent... it's far away."

Cari lifts her nose to the sky along with Hadrian and Virius. And then, in unison, all three of their gazes drop to the ground.

"Do you smell that?" asks Virius, his eyes glowing bright.

"I do," says Cari. "Whoever she is, she smells delicious."

"Whoever she is she has Gaius," says Hadrian.

A growl sounds in the night. It comes from Virius. "Whoever she is, she's mine."

32

———

G*aius*

"AHHH... ohhh... Oh my gods, Gaius, I never knew it could be like this."

I lean against the opposite side of the doorway as I watch Zahara bounce on the bed. She looks like a kid staying up late at a sleepover. Nothing like the porn star getting her back blown out that she's pretending to be.

"Don't stop." She bangs her hands against the rock face wall. "Don't stop. Ahhh."

I moan at the performance. It does not do my

abilities any justice. Just as I'm about to launch a formal protest, I hear movement from outside.

Zahara's eyes flash bright. She moves off the mattress. Her bare feet are quiet as she prowls across the room.

Though her feet are quiet, her mouth is not. She continues to make the cooing sex sounds. To me, she sounds like a cat in heat. An apt description, considering her animal nature.

She motions to me with her hand as she comes to one side of the door. I move into place at the other. But Zahara is still motioning. She points at her mouth, still making the mewling sounds, and then at my mouth. I groan but acquiesce.

"There you go, baby. Take my long cock all the way into that sweet pussy of yours as I fill it with my seed."

Zahara chokes on her mewls. Then she gags. Her face contorts into absolute horror and disgust.

What did she expect? I'm not an actor. My performance is based on real-life events. And it looks like my rendition has produced results.

The door begins to move. The fake sex reaches a climax as we both hold our breath. Up overhead, the moon is no longer sending light down the shaft. Sunrise is likely only an hour away. Or less.

A sliver of torchlight illuminates the cave. The crack opens wider. A hand reaches in. I grab it. I pull the man inside and crash his body against the wall.

"Zahara," shouts the male, "take him."

But Zahara doesn't take me; she takes the man. The male shifter has half a foot on her, but she still manages to wrap her claws around the back of his neck and pull his back flush to her chest. Her dagger is at his throat as she frogmarches him out of the room.

"Move," she commands.

I see five other males just outside the door. All of their gazes are menacing. All of their sharp claws are ready to tear flesh.

I am equal parts lover and fighter. Five women, I could please with some effort. Five males would be hard to kill on my own. Not to mention having to look out for a small female shifter with a sassy mouth and only a dagger.

"I never would've guessed it," says the captive leader. "You were always so frigid, but you get a little dick in you and it turns your pretty head."

"Of course you would think this was his idea," Zahara says, jerking her head back to me.

It galls me to stand behind a woman when violence is afoot, but unlike the male shifters, I can see that this pretty little head has thought all of this through.

"You let a colonizer in between your thighs and you forget your people, your mission."

I want to argue that I was born before the French sailed to the Americas. But that argument isn't paramount now. The sun's rays are waking, and I have to get on the other side of these men to get out of here.

"Oh, I haven't forgotten my mission, Hok'ee," says Zahara.

"Then take this dagger off my neck and point it at the leech."

The males surrounding us dig in their heels. None of them ball their fists. All splay their claws, ready for attack. But in their ready focus on the scene before them, they aren't looking behind them.

"This land belonged to our ancestors," Hok'ee goes on. "The white man stole it. But with your royal blood and this demon's seed, you will birth the Midnight Son and the land will become fruitful again. The prophecy says so. We can be rich."

"That's your problem, Hok'ee," said Zahara. "This has never been about the land for us."

"Us?"

Behind the men, dozens of cat eyes flash in the darkness. The women pounce on the males. Some turn fully into their animal forms of tawny yellow and black spots, or reddish-brown and black spots. The women outnumber the males, and the fight is over before it really began.

Zahara steps around Hok'ee, who was left unmarred, just a tiny prick at his neck from her dagger. Hok'ee drops to his knees, along with his other men.

"You really thought I was going to let you use my body for your gains?" Zahara scoffs as she cleans her dagger on the white shift she's wearing. "Misogyny is the colonialism of the twenty-first century."

If my heart wasn't already taken, I'd have a boner for her. There is nothing like the smell of a strong woman. My nose twitches as I catch the scent of another strong woman coming into the cave.

Marechal. She is here. But how?

Then I smell my brothers alongside Marechal's sweet scent. My entire world appears at the mouth of that cave. My brothers, my new siblings, and the love of my life.

But a pack of jaguar shifters stands between us, their claws unsheathed and ready to fight.

33

Marechal

So, vampires aren't going to be the only shock to my system tonight. There are big cats transforming into women before my eyes. It takes the meaning of being a cat lady to a whole new level. But I'm prepared to step through them because Gaius is on the other side.

As I take a step, I hear a low hiss coming from both animals and females. Upon closer inspection, these are not simply big pussycats that would sit in a ray of sunlight from the window.

These are jaguars, with sharp claws and pointy teeth.

"Lay a claw on her, and all bets are off."

I would never have suspected that such menace could come from Gaius Serrano's silky tone. From across the room, his eyes flash pure threat and destruction.

"I'll stay if you let them go."

His gaze is on me but he's talking to a woman standing at his side. I peer into the dimly lit room and make out Zahara. She isn't looking at Gaius. Her gaze is dead set on me.

"I already told you," she says, "you're not the one I want."

Zahara takes a step forward. The pack of women and big cats part to let her pass. Beside me, I feel movement. Virius, who had been standing in front of me like a shield, steps forward as well. His movements are stilted, as though he's being pulled to Zahara by some unseen force.

"We have no quarrel with the Durands." Zahara stops when she is an arm's length from Virius. "I want that one."

"You can't have him," say Hadrian and Gaius in unison.

"I'm not leaving here," says Virius.

The man stands toe to toe with Zahara. His height and bulk dwarf her, but to my eyes, they look on par with each other. I have known Zahara for years, but she doesn't look like the girl I knew. She looks like a force of nature. Now that I see the strength in her direct gaze, I can't remember that meek girl who bent over my vines. I wonder if she ever even existed.

Gaius comes up to the pair. Neither appears to notice him. Zahara is sizing Virius up as though he's the perfect specimen of grape that she's preparing to shear from the vine. Virius gazes at Zahara as though she is the sunlight reflecting off the dew of a budding vine.

"Viri—" Gaius tries, but his brother shakes his head.

"You and Hadrian tried to save me, tried to give me purpose," says Virius. "I'm a broken monster, but there is one thing I know how to do."

Virius turns from Zahara then. It looks like it pains him to do so. He turns to face Gaius. Hadrian comes up to the other side of him.

"Look at her," Virius says to his brothers. "She's so tiny and wee. She needs me to protect her."

Zahara scoffs at that. There's a dagger in her

hand and blood on her white dress. Exactly what has happened in here?

"Earlier, before he saw her, he called her his," says Hadrian.

"He's wrong," says Zahara. "He's mine. My captive, a sacrifice to appease the gods."

"A sacrifice?" says Viri. "Wouldn't be my first time. Do you have an altar? Cuffs? Rope? Anything but a stake, I'm okay with."

Zahara blinks rapidly as she stares at Virius. For the first time, her veneer of certainty cracks, and her gaze lowers.

"Don't worry, brother," says Virius. "This isn't a nightmare. I have a feeling I will sleep well from this day forward."

Hadrian and Gaius exchange another look. But in the end, they each give Virius a hug before leaving him with the women.

Gaius scoops me up into his arms and squeezes. Then I am flying through the air. When I open my eyes again, we are out of the cave. The moon is quickly sinking beneath the horizon.

"We have to get inside," says Hadrian.

Gaius bites his lip. His fang is sharp as it captures the flesh. I run my finger over the point, and he gasps.

"You know?" he says.

"I know," I say. "And when you wake up tonight, we're going to have a talk about what you did to my brother. We talk out our issues in this family, not make each other forget."

The laugh startles out of him.

"Somebody's in trouble," Cari singsongs.

"Oh, you are on my shortlist, too, missy. You lied to me."

Cari purses her lips. Then she spreads them into a wide grin, fangs and all. "Love you, Mare."

"I love you, too, *mon chou.*"

I pull my sister into a firm embrace. From the corner of my eye, I spot Arneis. His scowl swings between Hadrian and Gaius.

"So, are you going to wipe our minds again?" he asks. "Make Marechal and me forget what we just saw?"

"No," says Gaius. "You're both a part of this family now. We protect our own."

Arneis chews on that. But the corners of his mouth remain pinched, as though the taste is bitter. I am not looking forward to the next holiday dinner. The arguments around the table will be next level.

Still, my heart is happy. I have my family back. I

have my business back. And, for the first time, I've made space for love in my life.

Gaius wraps me in his arms and carries me inside. The sun is at his heels as he closes his bedroom door.

"Sleep with me," he says.

"For the whole day?" I've never slept the day away. It sounds irresponsible. It sounds like a plan. But that's not what Gaius has in mind.

"Not for the whole day. For your whole life."

34

———

G*aius*

HER HAND SLAPS MY CHEST. Her nails dig into my skin. My heart stops beating as my life flashes before my eyes.

I am afraid. Not of any pain. I am afraid of any emptiness that will result if Marechal refuses me.

"What are you saying, Gaius?" Marechal asks as her hand continues to press into me. "Are you asking me to marry you?"

Am I? I'm not certain. That doesn't sound like it would be long enough to get my fill of this woman.

"Marriage lasts a lifetime," I say. "I can offer you more than that."

Marechal's throat works as she gazes into my eyes. I could compel her, but her will is too strong. And the taste of her submission is far too tempting for me to give up.

"You want to make me like you? A vampire?"

"It's a dangerous process; too dangerous. You could die."

"What is the success ratio?" Marechal purses her lips. Her pupils dart as they calculate.

My fangs water as her mind whirs. "You're so fucking sexy when you talk maths."

A shy grin spreads across her face. My dick is hard for her. But it's my heart that is aching with need.

"We'll look at the statistics another time," I say. "For now, I just want your heart."

She places her hand on my chest. There is a scrap of fabric there. It smells of Virius. I spare a worry for my brother as I yank it away. When I see the blood there, my fangs protrude out of my mouth.

"Are you hungry?" she asks.

I try to swallow, but my teeth feel too big for my mouth. I don't want to scare her. But who am I kidding? This woman didn't flinch in a room full of jaguars. My unflappable boss bitch. Life with her is going to be a ride.

"Here." She tugs at the strap of her sundress, baring her shoulder. Then she pushes her dark hair aside, baring her neck.

Now my dick aches as much as my fangs. The adrenaline in my veins is burning. Yet, she is calm. That will not do. I want my first taste of her to be the perfect temperature of passion, pleasure, and bliss. And so I rip the garment from her body.

She is laid out bare before me. Her dark nipples are taut. Her cunny is already dripping with want. Already, she's sweet. But I want more.

I part her thighs. Using my shoulders, I force her legs wide. My mouth waters as I gaze at those perfectly plump lips.

Marechal jackknifes off the bed as my fang scrapes the soft skin where her leg meets her secret flesh. It's just a nip, an appetizer before I start my main course. I have little patience tonight, no finesse left.

I latch onto her pussy and begin to lave. Her body is so primed for me, so obedient to my dominance, that the first orgasm I pull from her is a simple affair. But it's enough to sweeten her blood. And I am thirsty.

Before she comes down, I bare my fangs. I lift my head to let her see the monster whose soul she's saved tonight. The man whose heart she now owns.

She doesn't scream. She doesn't flinch. She lets her head fall back in a move of submission.

The move nearly chokes the life out of me. I've made this strong woman surrender to me. I am humbled as her will bends. I am chastened as her back arches. But I am also hungry.

I sink my fangs into the femoral artery in her thigh. Marechal gasps, a long, low moan. Her body quakes as a second orgasm wracks her body. I plug her with my fingers so that she has something to cling to.

I pull deeply on her vessel, drinking heavily of her sweet, rich blood. Our hearts sync to the same beat. I have a feeling it will be that way for the rest of time.

The taste of her blood brings me to a climax of my own. My dick weeps in my pants as I drink her down. That has never happened to me before, and I can't wait to do it again.

But I can already feel the sun pulling me to sleep. Any more pleasure will have to wait until a new night. The room is secure, with blackout curtains to keep us safe.

I wrap Marechal in my arms, shielding her from any care, taking away any worry. But she wraps her arms tightly around me too, letting me know that I will never again have to shoulder a burden alone.

"Yes," she whispers, sleep tugging away at her consciousness.

"Yes, what *mon couer?*"

"That's my answer to your question. Yes, to all of it."

Don't miss Virius' story in
Her Vampire Knight.
Turn the page for a sneak peek!

EXCERPT OF HER VAMPIRE KNIGHT

Zahara

I stare at the beast's body as he stirs from his day's long sleep. He's not hairy like many of the four-legged prey I've hunted in the rainforests of Central America. But he is the biggest game I've taken down. Because Virius Serrano is a big male.

One of his arms is thrown over his forehead, holding back his thick blond curls. His other hand is flung out to the side, fingers flexing and curling as though lying in wait for a would-be attacker to come upon him. Little does he know he is already caught.

He walked into my trap just a half-day ago. In

fact, he willingly offered himself up to me in exchange for his brother's life. I'd say it was an honorable move, but I know better. There is no honor in the still hearts of vampires.

My gaze remains transfixed on my quarry. Virius wears a t-shirt featuring the Sioux warrior Crazy Horse. On his strong thighs, he wears cowboy chaps over the jeans that are molded to his form.

I take my time as my gaze takes in his package. Not because I find his form pleasing. I find the whole get-up offensive. Cowboys and Indians, really?

My father's people are of the Tohono Oodom tribe. My mother hails from the ancient Maya of Central America. It's not my indigenous tailfeathers that are ruffled. What flutters through my head like a butterfly flapping its wings on its nascent flight is how the man's chest fills out his shirt.

With each inhale, the hem of the t-shirt rises up higher and higher, giving me a view of the man's eight-pack. There is a tiny dusting of dark blond hair that extends from his belly button and disappears down the waistband of his jeans. The bulge there is clear through the fabric.

I'm supposed to make a baby with him.

The thought makes me cross my legs where I sit on the edge of the cot. The thought and the sight of the bulge in his pants are overwhelming. Yes, Virius Serrano is a very, very big boy.

I wouldn't call myself petite. But beside this golden-haired lion, I might as well be a house cat. I have no idea how this will work.

Yes, of course I know how sex works. I grew up around animals. I read a couple of romance novels. And I have Wi-Fi on my cell phone, though the little screen doesn't allow as much detail as I would like.

I know the mechanics of the textbook, step by step instructions. But I haven't followed the steps yet, mainly because none of the boys I grew up with would dare come near my sacred womb—or rather, my magical pussy as I started calling it after reading romance novels.

I place my hand over my flat belly. In just a few days' time, a baby will begin to grow in there. A child with even more responsibility than me. My womb is the vessel to break a curse.

I thought I'd had a rough time, being part American Indian and part Indigenous Mayan. Being raised with the traditional values of my people while lending an ear to modern feminist values. Being a human female with an animal living inside of her.

My unborn son will exist between two worlds as well. But his existence will be in the middle of two supernatural worlds. My son will be part jaguar shifter and part vampire.

There has never been such a pairing. It is completely unfathomable. But it was prophesied, and that prophecy is due to come to fruition in just a few nights.

In just a few nights, I will have to take this big man into my body. Have him move inside me like I've seen animals do in the field, pictures in textbooks, couples in movies.

I huff out an impatient breath. I've waited twenty-two years for this moment. All this build-up for nearly two decades. Then, in a matter of a couple of days, it will be over in a few moments, if the animals' couplings have taught me anything.

As though he could hear my thoughts, Virius jolts awake. His gaze immediately tracks to mine. Those honey-colored eyes hold me in place, leaving me in a situation I have never faced in my entire life. His gaze makes me feel as though I am the caught prey.

Which is ridiculous. He's my captive. He's about to bend to my will.

And then all I can think of is bending. Him bending me over and taking me from behind as I've seen it done in nature.

Virius's blond brow lifts. In amusement? In challenge? In acceptance?

I have the presence of mind to blush. Vampires can get into people's heads. Has he seen what I've been thinking about him?

His lips part. The top one, shaped in the bending curve of a heart, loosens from the lush bottom one. That bottom lip looks like the plumpest pillow I've ever seen. I want to lay my mouth against it—that is, until I see the bright gleam of fangs.

I shift on the cot, crouching into a fighting stance. A dagger is in my palm.

"I'm sorry," he says.

His voice is like the low grumble of a lion. I would have thought he was roaring at me before charging and taking me with those pointed teeth. The more shocking move is that I hold still.

Not because I want him to bite me, but because I've never before heard the words he's said; definitely not from a male.

"Did you just apologize?" I ask, not lowering my blade.

Virius takes a deep breath. He rubs his hands over his face, closing his eyes and leaning his head back. His jugular is exposed. He's presenting the most sensitive part of himself to my blade as though he isn't in the least afraid of me. When he pulls his hand away and straightens his head, the fangs are gone.

"I would never do anything to harm you, Zahara," he says.

It's the first time he's said my name. The way he forms the Z makes it trill like a string pulled on a guitar. It hums through me, making me vibrate until it reaches the R in my name. That becomes a caress that pulsates all the way down to my fingertips and toes.

He holds me still once more with those eyes. They shine so brightly that I can see everything in him. Does the man not know how to shutter his gaze? The eyes are truly the window to the soul, and he has left the door wide open for me.

Or maybe it's a trick. Maybe he's trying to mesmerize me. I blink and look away. But I still feel drawn to him, wanting to look back up and seek the heat of his gaze.

"I'm sorry that I had to sleep," he says. "The sun's pull on me is too great. I fought as long as I could to stay awake and protect you."

Protect me? "You do realize that you're a captive here?"

He looks around the room as though it's the first

time he's seeing it. The rumors about him all indicate that Virius… isn't quite right in the head. Something about the vampire who turned him being a sadistic Dominatrix from the old world.

"I'm holding you captive," I say slowly. "So, I don't need your protection. You're under mine."

Virius grins at that. For a creature who is allergic to the sun, his smile would be that star's greatest rival. "You are wee but mighty."

He called me that the other day.

Wee.

Like he's some Scottish highlander and I'm his lass.

I know he was a Roman soldier who'd later gotten his kicks in the Spanish Inquisition by first torturing and then drinking the blood of prisoners. And now he is squatting on my family's ancestral land. But once I am with child, the gods will see fit to right that wrong the American government thought they could erase with paper and pen. Which means there is no time like the present to get down to business.

"Listen, here's the deal," I say. "I'm holding you here until the eclipse, which is in a couple of days."

Virius nods, but I get the feeling he's not listening. His gaze is on my lips. His golden gaze flitting up, down, and across as I form words.

Subconsciously, I wet them. The tip of my tongue sneaks out and curls over my top lip. At the move, his nostrils flare. Something inside me heats, making my next words easy to say.

"We're going to have sex then. On the night of the eclipse."

Virius blinks. Then he frowns. He had been leaning slightly forward, towards me. Now he leans back, as far away from me as he can get.

That doesn't seem right. I'm sure he's into me. Most guys are into me. If they're not from my tribe, they look at me like I'm some exotic, brown treat they want to go slumming with.

Not Virius. He looks horrified at the thought of getting busy with me. Maybe vampires are immune to the magic sparking between my thighs?

"It's not my idea," I hurry to say. My wounded pride is doing backflips to put some distance between us. "It's part of the prophecy."

The prophecy that will break the curse of the land and return its rightful ownership to my people. Not that I truly care about that.

I mean, of course I want to claim my birthright. But what I want more is to stay here in the States.

Arizona has nothing on the beauty of Guatemala's rainforest. But the educational opportunities of these northerners are something that makes my mouth water.

"Is someone forcing you?" Virius asks, his voice going to a low register that warns of danger.

I like the way it rumbles through me. It coils and uncoils like a snake. The weight of it wraps around me, and something inside of me shivers.

"Because I will pull out his entrails through his arse and feed them to the bastard."

Well, that was certainly visual. At least I see that Virius's distaste has less to do with me than with the thought that I may be in danger.

"No," I say. "No one's forcing me. It's my destiny."

"Your destiny?"

"Yes."

Virius considers that. The hand he raked through his hair now scratches at the day's worth of stubble on his chin. "My answer is still no."

The dagger I forgot I was holding slips from my grasp. It clatters on the bed with a thud, resting between us. "No?" I ask.

"No," he confirms. "I will not have sex with you."

So, let me get this straight: I'm finally about to bag a guy who is not in my tribe, who doesn't look at my vagina like it's the holy grail, and he's telling me no?

Hunh?

Maybe I'm the one who is cursed.

Grab your copy to keep reading
Her Vampire Knight now!

ABOUT INES JOHNSON

Lover of fairytales, folklore, and mythology, Ines Johnson spends her days reimagining the stories of old in a modern world. She writes books where damsels cause the distress, princesses wield swords, and moms save the world.

If you liked Ines' Vampires, then you'll love her Dragons; alpha male shifters, fated mates, and steamy romance with a touch of 80's nostalgia! To grab a free book from the world of the Last Dragons just visit https://ineswrites.com/ReaderGroup

MORE PARANORMAL ROMANCE BY INES JOHNSON

Dark Vintage

Her Vampire Prince

Her Vampire Lord

Her Vampire Knight

His Vampire Princess

The Last Dragons

The Dragon's Reluctant Sacrifice

The Dragon's Ambivalent Sacrifice

The Dragon's Willing Sacrifice

The Dragon's Rebellious Sacrifice

The Dragon's Compliant Sacrifice

The Dragon's Forbidden Sacrifice

The Moonkind Series

Moonlight

Moonrise

Moonfall

The Knights of Caerleon

First Knight

One Knight

Arabian Knight